Hay and musk… Cowboy and all man.

She inhaled the scent of him, not stopping to think how crazy it was being a heartbeat away from kissing Jared Colton, the town cipher.

When his lips brushed hers, she groaned at the burst of electricity that sizzled in her veins. She dropped her hot-chocolate mug to the ground, and heard Jared do the same with his, just before he made a low sound in his throat, then cupped her face in his palms, deepening the kiss.

It was everything a first kiss should be, and a wave of yearning swept over Annette. Good and bad, because she didn't want this to stop, even though she knew it should.

There was something about Jared that made her throw caution to the wind, to forget about how she'd gotten to St. Valentine and why. To forget that she barely knew a thing about him.

All she knew was that she could stay there all night, in his arms.…

Dear Reader,

I wish St. Valentine, Texas, really existed, because I would love to stroll down the Old West boardwalks. I would love to have tea at the St. Valentine Hotel, too, and maybe even stay the night to meet some of its supposed ghosts! Mostly, I would love to meet the heroes and heroines of the books: Violet and Davis, Rita and Conn… and now Jared and Annette.

Yes, Jared is a lost soul, and Annette is running from her own problems. But they have true grit as they solve the mystery that started in book one about cryptic town founder Tony Amati. Love changes everyone, especially these two as they come together in the end. :)

If you like contests, you should stop by my website, www.crystal-green.com, and see what's cooking. Also, I'm now on Twitter at @CrystalGreenMe, so I'd love it if you said hi to me there, as well!

All the best,

Crystal Green

THE COWBOY'S PREGNANT BRIDE

CRYSTAL GREEN

HARLEQUIN® SPECIAL EDITION®

Recycling programs
for this product may
not exist in your area.

ISBN-13: 978-0-373-65723-0

THE COWBOY'S PREGNANT BRIDE

Copyright © 2013 by Chris Marie Green

Printed in U.S.A.

Books by Crystal Green

Harlequin Special Edition

§§*The Texas Tycoon's Baby* #2124
‡‡*Courted by the Texas Millionaire* #2188
‡‡*Daddy in the Making* #2219
‡‡*The Cowboy's Pregnant Bride* #2241

Silhouette Special Edition

*The Black Sheep Heir #1587
The Millionaire's Secret Baby #1668
†*A Tycoon in Texas* #1670
††*Past Imperfect* #1724
The Last Cowboy #1752
The Playboy Takes a Wife #1838
~*Her Best Man* #1850
§*Mommy and the Millionaire* #1887
§*The Second-Chance Groom* #1906
§*Falling for the Lone Wolf* #1932
‡*The Texas Billionaire's Bride* #1981
~~*When the Cowboy Said I Do* #2072
§§*Made for a Texas Marriage* #2093
§§*Taming the Texas Playboy* #2103

Harlequin Blaze

Innuendo #261
Jinxed! #303
"Tall, Dark & Temporary"
The Ultimate Bite #334
One for the Road #387
Good to the Last Bite #426
When the Sun Goes Down #472
Roped In #649

Silhouette Romance

Her Gypsy Prince #1789

Silhouette Bombshell

The Huntress #28
Baited #112

*Kane's Crossing
†The Fortunes of Texas:
  Reunion
††Most Likely To...
~Montana Mavericks:
  Striking It Rich
§The Suds Club
‡The Foleys and the McCords
~~Montana Mavericks:
  Thunder Canyon Cowboys
§§Billionaire Cowboys, Inc.
‡‡St. Valentine, Texas

Other titles by this author
available in ebook format.

CRYSTAL GREEN

lives near Las Vegas, where she writes for the Harlequin Special Edition and Blaze lines. She loves to read, over-analyze movies and TV programs, practice yoga and travel when she can. You can read more about her at www.crystal-green.com, where she has a blog and contests. Also, you can follow her on Facebook at www.facebook.com/people/Chris-Marie-Green/1051327765 and Twitter at www.twitter.com/ChrisMarieGreen.

To the hardworking staff of the Knight Agency.
Each one of you is a treasure. Thanks for everything!

Chapter One

When Annette Olsen saw the dark cowboy walk into the Orbit Diner, her heart rate nearly spiked through the roof.

And it wasn't only because he was a tall drink of water, dressed all in black from his worn boots to his jeans, to the belt with the shiny rodeo championship buckle, to his Western shirt and hat that tilted over his brow.

No, even though the enigmatic Jared Colton was enough to put steam into any woman's steps, Annette had been waiting for the man to stop by for his frequent early lunch because, oddly enough, she had come across something she was sure he was going to want.

She smiled at her only customers as she finished checking on them. "Just let me know when you're ready to pay up." Then she headed for the counter and ultimately the back room before Jared could sit in his usual stool by the glass-domed pies.

"Fancy seeing you here," she said lightly, passing right by him.

When his dark-eyed gaze lit on her, her pulse gave a brutal jerk. But she stilled it, as she always did.

It wasn't like she had much of a choice, not if she wanted to keep a sense of privacy and stay as far under the radar as she'd been doing these past months.

He gave her one of those lopsided grins of his, a boon that not many others in St. Valentine ever saw, probably because Annette never got into the quiet cowboy's business or asked him too many questions about why he had stayed around St. Valentine for so long.

She could appreciate a person with secrets, she thought. After all, she had more than enough herself.

"I thought I'd surprise everyone by varying my lunch routine," he said. "I'm impulsive that way."

She laughed at his facetiousness, and he did, too. His hat still rode low, giving a slight shadow to the rest of his face, but she could tell that he was running a look over her. The slow brush of tingles down her body didn't lie.

Before she could stop herself, she rested a hand over her belly, which she'd been trying to hide with a baggier waitress uniform.

She was seven months along, her belly just now popping, and she was trying so hard to keep anyone from knowing. Not yet, at least, because that was when people would start asking about the father.

Had Jared been looking hard enough at her to notice a weight gain? Was he about to ask a million questions that she'd been avoiding ever since she'd come to this town months ago, dirt flying out from under her tires, her wedding dress crumpled in a heap in the trunk of her Pontiac?

If her pulse had been jogging before, it was definitely racing now as she kept waiting for Jared to say something.

Anything.

Somewhere in the back of her mind, Annette heard the fifties-flavored Valentine's-inspired music playing low over the ceiling speakers, heard her only other customers telling her that they'd left cash for their bill and her tip on the table, then the dinging bell as they exited the diner.

Absently, she lifted a hand in goodbye to them, then turned her attention back to Jared.

But all he did was reach for the nearby heart-decorated tin bucket that held all the napkin-wrapped silverware.

If there was anyone else in St. Valentine who understood how precious privacy could be, it was Jared Colton. He'd proved it time and again while keeping to himself after wandering into town shortly before she had, just as much of a cipher as she tried to be, then turning his back on anyone who tried to poke into his reasons for being here.

Even though everyone did have a good idea just why Jared had stuck around.

Her gaze wandered to the hand-drawn pictures hanging above the service window: renderings playfully showing the town's past in the late 1920s and the stoic faces of the townspeople, including one who was a dead ringer for the cowboy sitting in front of her.

Was Jared related to Tony Amati, St. Valentine's upstanding town founder? If so, then why hadn't he admitted it to anyone?

She brushed off the questions, then went behind the Formica-topped counter. It would provide cover for her tummy, even if it was getting too far along to hide.

He was unwrapping his silverware, and when he merely said, "It'll be the usual for me today," she almost sank against the counter in pure relief. So he hadn't seen her swelling belly—or, at least, he wasn't about to comment on it.

But how long would that last?

After she signaled to the ponytailed, hippy-goateed cook behind the service window for "the usual," she fetched a glass, filled it with ice and cola, then gave it to Jared. She propped her foot on a step stool that she'd recently put under the counter to take some of the weight off her feet.

"I've got your usual," she said. "And I suppose you expect service to be extra special because you were such a big shot in the rodeo."

A shadow seemed to pass over him, yet it disappeared quickly enough.

He glanced around the diner, which was painted in turquoise and looked as if it'd been decorated by the Jetsons when they were in a hearts-and-flowers mood, then changed the subject whip-quick. "Apparently, I came during a lull today."

All right. So she'd already found out that he was a champion subject-changer months ago. But she had also done her fair share of avoiding a lot of topics ever since she'd left behind what's-his-name.

Okay, his name was Brett. She might as well take some power back from him and just say his damned name.

Brett the Turd. Turdy Brett. Brett Turdwell. She had a thousand names for him.

"This lull is a nice rest," she said. "We've been on fire around here lately."

"Tell me about it."

"It's amazing how many tourists can be attracted by a good mystery like Tony Amati's unsolved death." Violet and Davis Jackson, the owners of the town's small paper, had uncovered Tony's odd, unresolved demise months ago, after Jared had appeared in St. Valentine and excited everybody's interest with his doppelganger looks. The reporters had been after him for interviews, but he never gave any to them.

He took a drink, then said, "You know, every time I turn on the TV I see St. Valentine and Tony Amati. It's all over the place."

"And that's exactly what Violet and Davis want. So does the chamber of commerce, especially shortly before the Valentine's Day Festival." Annette only hoped that the town wouldn't get too much of a profile.

She couldn't afford it.

Subtly, she skimmed a hand over her stomach. *I'm going to make sure no one knows where we went.*

"One would think," she said, "that you don't like watching those profiles about Tony and St. Valentine."

He didn't say anything, just took another drink of soda, as secretive as ever.

"Okay, Mr. Strong but Silent," she said, grinning a little, "I guess you wouldn't be interested in something I dug up about Tony Amati this morning, then, would you?"

Now he put the cola down.

Gotcha.

With a tiny shrug, she went to the back room and dipped her hand in the patchwork purse she'd bought at some dime store back when she'd stocked up on cheap clothing and necessities with the only cash she'd had on hand before lucking into this job. She came out with a rectangular metal box wrapped in bulky oilcloth.

By the time she returned to Jared, he'd tipped his hat back so that she could see all of his face, which might not be considered handsome as much as strong and manly, with a square chin set off with a slight cleft and an eternal five o'clock shadow covering his lantern jaw and his cheeks. He had the type of nose that you'd see on Roman statues and the same type of body, too—hard and muscular, with a strength that made adrenaline fly through her veins.

But that's how she'd felt when she'd first met Brett, too—the all-American college quarterback and youngest son of the oil-rich Tulsa Cresswell family.

The man who'd raised a hand to her on their wedding day before she'd left him to eat her dust.

She put the package on the counter, but Jared merely stared at it.

"Go ahead," she said. "It won't bite."

Still, he glanced at her as if it might do just that. "What is it?"

"A brand-new car. I was in a giving mood when I bought it."

That got a chuckle out of him.

Out of patience, Annette unwound the material from around the box, then opened it. She unwrapped more oilcloth from the contents and presented him with the final product.

He looked at the journal, with its hard-crusted covers sandwiching the yellowed, swollen pages.

Annette put it on the counter again. "I like to do some gardening. It's a calming thing, but…well, that's not what you want to hear, is it? What matters is that I was digging deep to loosen the soil in a part of the yard I hadn't been using when I hit something in the dirt."

"This," he said.

"A journal. And I peeked inside, just to see what it was, but when I got a load of Tony Amati's name written on the front page…"

"It's…Tony's?"

The question was infused with a quality she'd never heard from this man before—almost a hopeful vulnerability.

Had she and the rest of the townsfolk been wrong about him? Did he have more than a passing interest in Tony Amati?

She lowered her voice, even though Declan the cook was busy in the kitchen, judging from the faint noise of pots and pans. "I rent one of the condominiums they built on Tony's old ranch property, and I suppose he buried this journal at some point. Who knows why? It could give a reason in that journal, but I didn't have time to read it before work to find out. I'm curious like you wouldn't believe, but I thought maybe you should have the honor of looking at it first—"

Jared grasped the book in his big hands and opened it, just as if he'd been waiting for this moment his entire life.

The first thing Jared saw was a fine scrawl of semi-blurred ink on the front page.

Amati.

And that's all it said. That's all it *had* to say in this town because everyone knew who Tony Amati was, even though no one seemed to have known him well.

He'd been a former Texas Ranger who'd struck oil in the late 1920s, founded St. Valentine and acted as a patron to those who needed jobs. A man who'd lived alone, shut away on his ranch. A taciturn guy who'd died without much more fanfare than a dutiful obituary in the local paper.

Ever since Jared's initial glimpse of Tony Amati's picture in the Queen of Hearts Saloon months ago, he'd known that he'd finally found what he'd been looking for all these years—roots, a possible identity.

Maybe even family?

But Jared had no proof of that, just a suspicion, based on the similarity of his and Tony's faces. After he'd left the rodeo circuit (too old and broken to be busting broncs after he'd tweaked his back during a tumble) and after he'd drifted from ranch to ranch and job to job for three years afterward (too ornery to be content in one place), he hadn't known where he was going or why. Yet, for once, Tony had given him a reason to linger.

He rested his fingertips on the first page, right by Tony's last name. He smiled.

Annette's soft voice floated to him. It was a sound that never failed to stir Jared, whether that was a good thing or not.

"Are you going to read it right now?" she asked.

"I could."

He looked up at her, and she grinned at him, her deep blue eyes sending those same swirls of heat from his chest to his belly. God, she was a sight, even in a pink waitress uniform and white apron. It was as if she didn't belong in a diner—she seemed too well-bred for it for some reason he couldn't put his finger on. She had a way of carrying herself that made him think more of champagne parties and diamond rings than coffee and flatware.

Sometimes she wore her long, wavy, light blond hair down, the ends brushing the middle of her back. But not today. She'd put her hair in a bun with a pencil stuck out of it.

Damn, what Jared would give to slip that pencil out of her hair and watch it tumble down, allowing him to bury his fingers in it. She was like a Nordic princess to him, her rosy cheeks hinting at her obvious youth and telling him that she couldn't be older than her early twenties. She was tall and slender. Her cheekbones were high, her lips full, her jaw sculpted enough to make him want to trace it.

Yeah. As if that was ever going to happen. Jared had made a career out of keeping a distance, and it'd have to stay that way, especially because he could've sworn that he'd noticed an extra curve to her today.

Her belly.

Maybe he was making too much of it, but the bump on Annette had reminded Jared of a series of painful times, like when he'd been awakened late at night by his uncle Stuart, who'd taken him back to his ranch after his parents had died in a freak train wreck.... Like when Jared had, years later, accidently come across a letter in Uncle Stuart's office from the man he'd thought to be his birth father—a letter mentioning that Jared had been adopted... Like how he'd felt a void after that, leaving the ranch just as soon as he could to travel the rodeo circuit, where he'd found a new family who seemed to understand that sometimes a man liked to keep a distance...

Like how he'd foolishly and quickly gotten married soon afterward. He'd been much too young, much too desperate to fill the emptiness that had spread inside him after he'd found out that he wasn't who he thought he was.

Most of all, there was the day his ex-wife had told him, *You're going to be a daddy.* And in the next breath, *It's too dangerous for a father to be in the rodeo, busting those broncs, Jared....*

But he'd loved the rush of those eight seconds on the back of a bucking horse too damned much—it was really the only time he felt full and alive—and he'd argued with her. His attitude had been enough to push Joelle away, into another man's arms—a good man, just like Tony Amati had been and just like Jared hadn't.

His selfishness had been enough to let him know that he wouldn't have made a good dad anyway, so he had let his ex-wife and daughter be because his ex had asked him to do just that.

A man of habit, he'd clung to the rodeo, staying on for a while longer, until he'd been thrown from that last bronc. It was a young man's sport, and thirty was too old to be competitive. So there he'd been—without a wife, without a child, without the rodeo that had given him some definition. And all he had was the memory of his adopted father's letter to haunt him.

But when Uncle Stuart had passed on and given Jared the ranch—a property that Jared had sold off—he had succumbed to a curiosity that had nagged him, even as he'd tried to stow it away, and hired a P.I. to find his birth parents.

It'd probably been the second-worst choice of his life.

You shouldn't have come here.... I don't even know who your dad is.... I gave you up so I wouldn't have to see you....

As with most everything else, Jared had stashed the memory of his birth mother far down, to a dark area that he shut nice and tight. Yet something had recently nudged it open a crack—the thought that, if he was related to Tony Amati, the saint of St. Valentine, his mother wouldn't matter.

He could really start to have something in St. Valentine. To have some*one,* and with Tony, it would be in the distant way he preferred.

In Tony's photos, Jared could see the better version of himself, and that's why he'd stayed in this town—to find out who he was.

Now, from across the counter, Annette glanced behind her. The cook wasn't at the service window, and when she turned back around, she had a conspiratorial expression on her beautiful face, nodding at the journal.

"Just read it now, would you?" she said.

He didn't need any more urging, and he turned to the first full page, scanning it eagerly.

Some men keep ledgers of their assets. Some men draw maps of their properties. Some write of their confessions so they might weigh less heavily in the inevitable end.

Though I should probably lift the burden of all my terrible sins from my shoulders within these pages, I...

Jared stopped cold, tripping over three words he hadn't been expecting.

My terrible sins...

He closed the journal just as Declan appeared in the service window with a plate of food, ringing the bell to signal that Jared's ham on rye with fries was up.

Annette thanked the cook, then grabbed the plate as he left, sliding it onto the counter as Jared placed the book on his lap, where the counter hid it.

It was obvious that she understood his gesture—she thought that he didn't want anyone else, like Declan, to see the journal and start asking questions about it. And that's why he liked Annette—because they didn't have to talk too much to get each other.

Annette's gaze shined. "Anything good so far?"

My terrible sins...

Jared shrugged. "I only got halfway down the first page." And, even now, he wasn't sure he was going to like what he saw in the rest of the journal. But there was an unidentifiable urge building in him to continue, just like the one that had pushed him to hire the P.I. to find his birth parents.

What did Tony mean by "terrible sins"?

And what if the town reporters, Violet and Davis Jackson, who were so bent on reporting every blamed thing about Tony Amati, found out about all the details before Jared could?

He imagined his ex-wife's rounded belly before she'd left him, imagined what his daughter might look like today, eleven years old, all knees and elbows and sugar and spice, and he tightened his fingers on the journal. Jared knew what it was like to be utterly devastated by a parent. His birth mom had made him wish he'd never found her. If his own daughter heard about her birth dad and his real family's "terrible sins," would she be just as dismayed?

Or worse, would she hardly care?

Letting go of the journal, he told himself it didn't matter. He'd left well enough alone with his daughter, Melissa, merely sending money to her mom each month. Even if he tried to get in touch with her—as he'd seriously thought of doing out of pure guilt, just after that P.I. had found his birth mother and Jared had hired him to find a few other loose ends—she would be old enough to refuse his phone calls. Old enough to hate him.

Annette cocked her head, reading him. "You look lost, cowboy."

Why did it sound as if she knew just how lost a person could be?

"Not lost," he said. Maybe it was time to leave now.

But he didn't. He stayed planted in his seat, with a slow, wistful Nat King Cole song playing on the sound system, with him longing to tell someone like Annette everything because he'd been holding it all in for so long.

It felt as if they were the only two people in the world, much less the diner.

Still, he couldn't bring himself to say a word. Why would she give a damn anyway about someone like him—a drifter? A wild card no one really knew?

Annette came out from behind the counter, going to

the table where her customers had left their bill and cash and then moving to the register to ring up the sale. "You had a look in your eyes, like you were thinking extra hard. Like you were thinking about disappearing out of here, just like you do most days in your truck, in the opposite direction of your job on the Harrison ranch."

It was the first time she'd ever gotten remotely into his business, and he found that he didn't mind it so much.

"Does everyone send out a special bulletin when I even sneeze?"

She closed the register as he turned in his seat to face her, propping an arm on his leg.

She looked encouraged by the fact that he hadn't shooed her off, as he did with certain reporters or nosy townsfolk. "You can tell me where you go."

He checked the service window. Declan was still AWOL, and it was just Jared and her.

Aw, what the hell.

"I've got a grandma just out of town," he finally said.

He didn't add that the P.I. had tracked down his maternal grandmother because Jared had been curious about any living relatives around the area. She'd been the reason he'd stopped in St. Valentine in the first place and ended up at that saloon, where he'd seen Tony's picture.

"How sweet," Annette said, coming to the counter again, this time dragging a chair from near the register with her so she could sit in it. So close, yet so far. "You visit your granny all the time. Who would've thought?"

He could smell Annette's perfume. Lilies? He hadn't paid attention to flowers in a long time.

"I might show this to her," he said, holding up the

journal. "She's kind of a historian, likes telling stories. But when I told her about my twin—" he nodded up at the Tony Amati picture "—she didn't let me know much."

And she'd gotten a strange look when he'd mentioned Tony's name, making Jared suspect that there was way more to her stories than she was letting on.

Annette was still bright-eyed. "Sometimes grandmas and grandpas know everything about a place. I didn't know either of mine very well, but..."

She trailed off.

"But..." he said because Annette rarely talked about her own personal life. He'd never asked her to.

"You're changing the subject," she said. "You're pretty good at that."

He wasn't the only one.

"Anyway," she said. "Your grandma...?"

"She said that she hadn't seen a picture of Tony in a long while so she couldn't comment on a resemblance."

"And when you told her that you two could've been brothers?"

"She said it has to be a coincidence."

"Oh." Annette frowned. "It's definitely a marked coincidence."

He thought so, too, but that's where he left the conversation. He didn't need to add that his suspicions about Tony were so strong that he'd checked into the St. Valentine Hotel at first, poking around the fringes of town in local libraries and on the internet, doing his own seemingly dead-ended research because he was too broke now to hire a P.I. Then he'd gotten a job and rented a cabin on the outskirts of town until he could get more answers.

The bell on the door rang as new customers entered. Obvious tourists, with their Grand Canyon sweatshirts and white city sneakers.

Annette went to wait on them, and Jared got to his lunch. The fries were fairly cold by now, but it didn't much matter. Not when Annette passed by and gave him one of her pretty smiles.

He finished his grub, stood and put enough cash on the counter to take care of the bill, plus a nice tip for Annette.

It was his day off from work, but that didn't mean there was any rest for the wicked, he thought, tucking the journal under his arm as he canted his hat to Annette.

"Thanks again for the gift," he said.

"Thank *you*." She held up his bill and grinned, then put the folder into her apron pocket as she went to the customers' table to take their order.

He watched her, positive now that he could make out a definite bump under her apron as clear as day.

But Jared's smile tamed itself as he thought of his own child, and he walked away just as he had the first time, something foreign gnawing at the edges of his heart.

Chapter Two

I never meant to fall in love with her. She is young—eighteen—while I am a man of thirty-five with a past that clings to me like an attached shadow, ready and waiting to tap me on the shoulder....

Jared set Tony's journal down on the seat beside him as he sat in his green Dodge truck on Horizon Road, the cracked blacktop stretching through lanes of fences. Around him, pastures dotted by trees reflected a February late afternoon, the branches like stark bones against the gray, rain-heavy sky.

He hadn't made it too far out of the old town before he'd choked off the truck's engine and opened the journal, fueled by curiosity as he scanned it. He'd even made it through the entire thing, but...

This passage. It was the one he would come back to time after time, as if it were tar that sucked at his boots, keeping him from continuing.

My terrible sins...

A past that clings to me like an attached shadow...

He couldn't get those phrases out of his head. And they frustrated the hell out of him because, as it turned out, the journal was filled with vague statements like these. In fact, the book was actually more of an outlet for a side of Tony that Jared had never expected: a lovelorn man who'd scribbled his innermost thoughts down over the course of a few months, as if the pages were the only things he could talk to.

And by the last page, when there should've been so many answers about who Tony was and what exactly those terrible sins of his were...

The entries just ended.

Par for the mysterious Tony's life, huh?

Jared gave the journal the stink eye. As much as he was interested in this nameless woman Tony had crushed on way back when—and Jared already had a guess as to who she was—he wanted to know the nitty-gritty. The past Tony kept referring to. The confessions he should've been making.

Then again, there was a part of Jared that didn't want to know the man's dirty deeds at all because Tony the saint—and Jared's possible great-grandfather—had a hold on him that wouldn't quit.

To think, he would've finally been proud of something in his life besides the championship rodeo belt buckle he wore—an object that seemed more tarnished than anything to Jared.

He stared down the road out his windshield, which was speckled with a few stray drops of rain.

So Tony had a few sins. What if all his good deeds overcame everything else about the man?

Jared shook his head. He had always looked out for the shadows instead of the sunlight—it was how he'd been raised by Uncle Stuart, an emotionally inaccessible man. Sure, Stuart had gruffly seen to it that Jared had everything he needed, but he hadn't been a real parent, and he'd seemed to be keenly aware of that. He'd never even tried to live up to the title, leaving four-year-old Jared in a room down the hall shortly after his parents had passed on, his blankets pulled up around his neck, his brain refusing to let him go to sleep because of all the shadows on the walls and all the things out there that would get to a person, whether it was a trick of the nightlight making warped shapes near the closet door or even a nightmare about a train that went off the tracks.

Jared had learned early on to be tough, to close his eyes until his heartbeat smoothed out. To hold back the tears and take care of himself rather than call to his uncle for help, even though Stuart had told him that he could.

Yes, growing up, Jared had learned to distance himself from fear and love because both could disappear if you just closed your eyes.

But this time…shouldn't he open them, just to see if there was something else out there besides the shadows, like the love Tony had recorded in his journal? What if Tony *was* related to him and it turned out that he didn't really have much as far as "terrible sins" went?

Jared longed to find out, to maybe even believe that a good man like Tony might've welcomed him into the family more than his granddaughter, Jared's birth mom, had.

He took his gaze off the book, tapping his fingers on his steering wheel. He could see the cluster of brick condo buildings through the dots of rain on the glass.

The complex they'd built on Tony's old ranch property.

Annette had told Jared that she'd dug up the journal in her garden. What were the chances that old Tony had buried more there?

Family documents? Pictures? Another journal in which he actually let those terrible sins off his chest?

And what were the odds that Annette might have finished her early shift at the diner by now?

A burst of fire roared through his veins. That shiny moon-blond hair, her creamy skin, her lips…

Jared chuffed and wiped a hand down his face. His mind—or whatever it was—didn't belong on a woman. He'd had his share of them in the past, both buckle bunnies and cowgirls, and he'd overstayed his welcome only once. It'd been a mistake he was still living with.

Yet, all he needed from Annette was access to that garden of hers.

He sat there for a while longer—time enough for him to turn on the radio for a marathon of country songs. Time enough for him to tell himself that he should probably just drop this and move on.

But then, through the dusk, he saw a bright red Pontiac pulling into the complex and passing the iron gates with a rustic arch that spelled out *Heartland*—the name of Tony Amati's original ranch.

Jared rested a hand on his door latch. Didn't Annette

drive a Pontiac? He'd seen it in the parking lot every time she worked.

He blew out a breath.

This was crazy. Was he really thinking of going through with this ridiculous mission?

Then he opened the door. Hell, yeah, he was thinking of it. He hadn't stayed in St. Valentine because of the meatloaf or ham sandwiches. Or because of the gorgeous blonde who served them.

Right?

As a niggling thought permeated him, he shook it off, pulled his dark shearling coat out of the truck cab, then shut the door. The air smelled as if the earlier rain had made everything new, and that made him think that maybe this was a better idea than he'd first thought.

He ambled to a rose-lined walkway that led to a gate in a brick wall. At the same time, he pulled up the collar of his coat, minding the threat of the moody sky. Up ahead, the walk was sprinkle-damp, and yellow lights from condo windows beckoned.

One of them was Annette's.

As he shut the gate behind him, he corrected himself. *I'm not looking for Annette, just a certain garden patch.*

He came to a bricked cove with a bank of mailboxes, each with a last name posted on it. But there were no corresponding numbers for the condos.

Okay, then. No worries. He would just continue on his way, and he might run into Annette coming out of her garage or a parking space.

So he went right on ahead. But…

What would he say to her exactly?

How-de-do, I just happened to be in the neighborhood. And, really, I'm not a weird stalker. I'm only

*interested in doing some archeological work in your
backyard.*

How lame would that sound?

He almost turned around right then and there, except that's when he caught sight of some movement in a lower-level window and saw...

My God—a silhouette half-hidden through the sheer mist of yellow curtains.

Jared's heart slammed into his ribs, and he couldn't take another step because he could feel it in his bones—it was Annette.

Yeah, he should've averted his eyes, but the light was coming from behind her, showing her in a haloed, curvy profile without that waitressing apron that had covered her belly today. Now, without it, there was very clearly a bump in plain view.

A baby.

After she took a step toward the window, apparently to draw the shades, she came into full sight.

She hesitated, then tenderly eased both of her hands over her tummy, sliding them beneath it to cup the child growing within it.

Jared's chest felt pierced, lanced by an ache.

She obviously already loved that child. But where was the father?

Where were you when your own daughter probably asked the same thing?

Feeling shamed, both because he'd witnessed such a private moment and because of his failures, he fisted his hands and got out of there before she saw him.

Before work the next day, Annette took a moment to soak her feet, then massage them before she had to stand on them all day at the diner. She'd done the same thing last night before going to bed, and she knew it wouldn't be long before she'd be craving a foot spa 24/7—and before she would have to significantly cut back on her hours at the diner or take a leave of absence altogether.

Rest, healthy eating and some pampering—that's what the doctor had ordered when she'd gone to him early in her pregnancy. She'd chosen a practitioner in the new part of town because it was more modern, relatively more crowded and less personal there.

She meant to make good on all the doctor's suggestions this morning, so she'd eaten scrambled eggs and a yogurt parfait with fresh fruit, granola and almond slivers for breakfast, then left her home an hour before her shift. That gave her enough time to run a couple of errands around the Old West streets of the Old Town portion of St. Valentine. The weather-beaten buildings contained things like a mercantile store and boutiques geared toward tourists. There were even burros roaming around—descendants of the beasts of burden owned by the silver miners who'd once lived here.

Now, of course, the silver mines were gone, along with the kaolin mine that had replaced them, and that's what had put St. Valentine in the economic dumps. But matters were improving, she thought as she rested on a bench in the town square after dropping by the general store for a few necessaries. And judging from the decent number of tourists she knew would be descending on Old Town and the diner in about a half hour, St. Valentine was rising once again.

She lifted her chin, letting the crisp morning air tweak her cheeks. Truthfully, St. Valentine had Jared to thank for their resurrection. It'd been his appearance that had stirred up interest in Tony Amati and alerted Violet and Davis Jackson to his mysterious death, which had taken place on the same night old Sheriff Hadenfield's home had been burglarized.

From the church, the sound of the recently restored bells tolled through the cleared-up sky, marking the hour. Outside, some people were decorating the trellises in the yard with white-flowered streamers.

A wedding.

Images crept back to Annette: reflections of a bride in a mirror, her Grace Kelly gown so white that no one would ever guess the results of the pregnancy test she'd just taken. Pictures of a woman who couldn't keep the news to herself and had rashly left her dressing room intending to tell her husband-to-be that they were going to be parents.

Nightmares of what she'd found when she'd opened his door, only to find him *en flagrante delicto* with a bridesmaid. And then…

Apologies from him after he'd sent away her friend. Yeah, a "friend," for God's sake.

Then the worst of it. A flash of his hand rising in the air after the bride had the temerity not to accept all his excuses and then call off the wedding.

"You look a little lost," said a man's voice.

It shocked Annette, partly because she hadn't expected anyone to be nearby, but mostly because she recognized who it was and because he left a twist of need spiraling through her.

She looked up to find Jared standing there in his black coat with Tony Amati's journal tucked under his arm.

Her blood surged, sending her pulse scampering.

"Isn't that supposed to be my line?" she asked, putting a smile on her face for him.

He smiled back in that lopsided way that took the edge off him. Then he gestured toward the bench.

"May I?"

She scooted over and pulled her long felt coat around her, as if that would protect every vulnerable angle he'd just seen.

But it didn't do any good—not when she could smell the hay scent of him, even over the fresh air, and surely not when she was all too aware of his broad shoulders under that coat.

He tilted up the brim of his hat, and she couldn't take her eyes off his strong profile.

"I think I got a little lost yesterday myself," he said.

"In the diner?" she asked, remembering their conversation after he'd first looked in the journal. He'd definitely seemed lost enough for her to have commented on it.

"Not in the diner." He laughed. "I'm embarrassed to admit that I got it into my head that your garden would be some kind of burial place for more Tony Amati artifacts. So I drove out there, hoping to just knock on your door and see if you'd let me do a little Indiana Jonesing."

Her skin flushed, just as if he'd spread fire over it. "You paid me a visit?"

"Before my better sense got to me, yes. I did."

A feeling of warmth and excitement expanded in her, and the awareness spilled over, alerting her to their proximity on the bench. Only a small space separated them. If she would only move her hand an inch, she would feel a vibration from his leg, a sense of being closer to him than ever.

What if she dared?

She didn't. The last thing she needed was to get involved with a guy she knew next to nothing about. A guy who rattled her as Brett had first done with his own manly presence, and look how that had turned out. She was better off not trusting her first impressions.

Besides, her baby needed more than a drifter. Actually, all her child needed was her, not any man at all.

Jared must have interpreted her silence as wariness, and he grabbed the journal from under his arm. "I ended up going home and rereading this entire thing in depth last night. It changed my mind again about approaching you." He offered it to her. "There's not a heck of a lot in here unless you're looking for a love story, so I'm hoping to find more—even if it's in your garden."

She took the journal. "Just like a man. If there aren't explosions and car chases, you're not interested."

"I'm interested, all right. I just didn't expect Tony to be..." He motioned with his hand.

"A sap for love?"

"Maybe." He paused. "All he talks about is some girl he fell for."

"I'd ask if he married her, but I know Tony never took a wife."

"Right. He wrote about how they met in secret all the time. She was engaged to marry someone else, though Tony says she didn't love him."

"She was a bad girl? How progressive for the time."

"Nah, from what Tony says, she was an angel. But her father disapproved of him, and it wasn't because of their age difference. Evidently, Daddy thought Tony didn't 'suit' his daughter."

"Ooh—a forbidden romance." She wanted to ask

if Tony had "gone digging in the girl's garden," but there were limits to flirting, especially with someone like Jared.

He leaned back, resting his arms on the top of the bench. His coat brushed her shoulder and she shivered.

"It's weird, though," he said. "Tony never wrote about the…details when it came to him and his girl."

"Details?"

Jared raised an eyebrow, and she understood.

Intimacies, she thought, thankful that Jared hadn't put it out there.

Was he feeling the tense atmosphere between them, too? Did he want to avoid it just as much?

He went on. "Tony doesn't even give her name. It's not that kind of notch-on-the-bedpost journal."

"What kind is it then?"

"The type of crap Romeo would've written about. You know, 'What light through yonder window breaks?' That sort of flowery stuff."

Annette playfully narrowed her eyes at him. "You know your Shakespeare."

"No, I don't." He looked disinterested. "I just had to read it freshman year in high school. The girls in class had this thing where they'd go around quoting it whenever they were sighing over some guy."

And how many of those girls had quoted lines about him?

"Anyway," he said, once again the persistent subject-changer, "you can read the journal if you want to, but later, after I show it to my grandma. I owe you that much for bringing it to me. But, if you do take it, I'd ask that you keep it out of sight."

Annette didn't know how to respond. He'd said it so

casually, but she got the feeling that letting her in on this was a big deal for Jared Colton.

She treated his gesture with the respect it deserved. "I'll do just that, Jared."

At the sound of his name coming from her, he met her gaze. It was as if his irises had heated to dark fire, and she had to glance back down at the journal to keep from getting scorched.

Without looking at him, she said, "And if you want to do some digging, you're welcome to come over to my place."

Because it was no big deal, right? Besides, she meant digging in the sense of "investigative labor," not...well, "digging in her garden."

His voice lowered, scratching over her skin. "Then I'll do that. Dig, I mean."

What precisely did *he* mean by "dig"?

Whatever it was, she would avoid it. He could be a friend, and that would be easy enough because she got the feeling he'd be leaving just as soon as he satisfied himself about Tony Amati for whatever reason.

That made everything pretty simple.

He stood, reaching out a hand to help her to her feet. When she grabbed it, a blast zipped up her fingers, heating her hand, her arm. Her chest.

Everywhere.

"I'm off work tomorrow if that suits you," he said. "Maybe I could drop by sometime early?"

Based on his regular appearances at the diner, he had to know that tomorrow was her day off, too. But she had some baby furniture being delivered at nine, and she didn't want him there to see proof of her condition. Not before she was ready for the dirt to hit the fan in this town and for her to have to tidy up all the growing lies she would have to tell.

"How about eleven?" she asked, going for something a little later than an early-rising cowboy probably had in mind.

"Sounds like a plan."

They hadn't disconnected hands yet, and when she realized it, she stepped away, finally distancing herself.

Her skin still burned, though. Wanting, needing.

She gave him back the journal, and when he started to walk away, the hunger didn't ease off, as her stomach tumbled with what had to be a thrill.

Suddenly she found herself asking him something better left unasked.

"Just why is it so important that you find out everything you can about Tony?"

His shoulders stiffened as he paused. But then he shrugged, and he almost pulled it off, too, except for the way his smile seemed strained.

"It's not important," he said as he lifted a hand in farewell, then sauntered toward his truck parked near the entrance to the mercantile, where he'd probably be filling it with supplies for the Harrison ranch.

It was the first obvious lie he'd ever told Annette, but she reminded herself that it was for the best.

She should be grateful for the distance he was putting between them, step by step.

And heartbeat by wistful heartbeat.

After Jared had banked some hours on the Harrison ranch, doing maintenance around the stables, he headed for dinner at Gran's house.

She lived in what he thought of as a gingerbread cottage, with brown planked walls and white trim around the doors and windows. He'd found out that the hand-painted decorations on the flower boxes under the windows had been done by his grandpa, back in the day, before his heart attack had left Gran alone for going on ten years now.

When he knocked, it took her a few minutes to answer, but he knew she'd get around to it just fine.

And when she did, she had a smile on her face as she opened her arms to him and gave him a great big hug.

"It hasn't been but a few days, but I missed you silly," she said as she pulled away, lifting her hands to pat his cheeks.

Jared hadn't ever had his cheeks patted like that before, and he felt his face going red. Gran thought that was pretty funny, and she had a good laugh.

He waited her out, still cautious around her because he'd never had a grandma before. His adoptive mom and dad had been older, both orphaned, and that's why Uncle Stuart, who'd never planned to have kids, had taken him in. In his own way, he had shown Jared that he wasn't very wanted.

He supposed that's why Tony held such an appeal for him—the man wasn't here to ever turn him aside, whereas a real-live grandma just might turn Jared away someday.

When she was done with her chuckles, she waved him inside, where it smelled like gingerbread, too. And casserole. And mothballs. But it was a comforting combination of smells that had already grown on him as much as he would ever allow it to.

"Take a seat," she said, gesturing to a battered recliner that had seen better days.

She settled on the worn doily-decorated sofa next to him, pouring sodas into waiting glasses, just as efficient as always.

She'd already donned a flowery housedress, as if it was a gown she used for entertaining guests—or, conversely, as if she'd become so used to him that she didn't mind what she wore when he came over. Her silver hair was in a low ponytail, and she was far too delicate to resemble a cowgirl who'd once helped to run a ranch with her husband before they sold it off years ago.

He set the oilcloth-wrapped journal on the table, and she stopped pouring.

"I thought I saw you bearing a gift, Jared, but I'm more of a roses or chocolates woman." She touched the oilcloth. "Just what is this?"

"I asked the same thing yesterday when a friend brought it to me." He explained who it belonged to and why his friend had found it in her garden.

It didn't take Gran but a second to pounce on the item. Her creased forehead told him that she was worried about the contents.

"Don't fret," he said. "I didn't find out a whole lot about the man."

"I'm not fretting." But she used her finger to help her speed through each line of each page anyway.

While she did that, Jared drank his soda. He even grabbed the remote to turn on the old TV and flip through the channels.

He wanted to ask Gran if she wouldn't mind getting out all the old photo albums she'd shown him over the months. Pictures of her wedding to his grandfather, images of Grandpa as a dimple-cheeked blond child.

Photos of Grandpa's mom, Tessa Hadenfield, in particular, with her blond hair and dimpled, spritely smile.

When Gran was done reading, she took the remote from him and turned off the tube. She was no longer frowning.

"Find anything worrisome?" he asked.

"Hardly. I kept a diary when I was younger, too, but I was a teenager. Tony must not have had many friends to talk to."

"Just the journal."

"He was terribly sweet on whoever this girl was, though. That's clear."

And doesn't that make you connect any dots? Jared thought. *Isn't there a possibility that Tony and this girl got together even outside of marriage and had a kid, and that kid had their own child, and then...that child had* him?

Even more to the point, because the P.I. who'd directed him to Gran had told him that she was his maternal grandmother, Jared suspected that Tony had perhaps fallen in love with his great-grandmother Tessa, who'd been the sheriff's daughter.

And the woman who'd gotten married to someone who wasn't Tony.

Was that what Tony meant whenever he mentioned terrible sins?

But Jared knew it was fruitless to ask Gran about all this because, for whatever reason, she wouldn't talk about Tony in anything but broad strokes.

So Jared took the less obvious route.

"Who do you think the woman was?" he asked.

"Tony's dreamboat? I have no idea."

Uh-huh. Jared knew lies from truths, and this was a

prime example of the former. But he also knew his gran by this time, too, because he'd spent several months in her company at their weekly dinners.

She wasn't going to give up anything to him she didn't want to.

When she popped out of her seat to see to the meal, Jared took the journal in his hands again, opening it to another passage that he'd lingered over last night.

She's an angel, and when the sunlight catches her hair, it's as if I can catch a glimpse of a found paradise....

And, just like last night, Jared couldn't help but picture a woman who resembled his own blond angel, even though he didn't have a devil of a chance with her.

Chapter Three

Well, isn't this the story of my life? Annette thought as Jared arrived moments before the baby furniture delivery guys wrapped up their business in her condo.

Always with the bad timing.

He was at her open door, stopping at the threshold after the delivery man from a store in New Town carried in a box to the second bedroom.

Jared removed his hat, revealing black hair that was so thick and wavy it made her melt.

"Am I interrupting something?" he asked.

All she could do was shrug. "My delivery was late. I was hoping—"

"That I wouldn't be here to see this?"

"Pretty much."

A second delivery man saved her when he came up to her with a slip to sign. When they left, she beckoned

Jared all the way inside, took his coat and hat, and put them on her dining table.

Capital A *awkward,* she thought. She'd scheduled the delivery when she knew the bulk of her neighbors, most of whom had jobs in the more modern New Town, would be at work. And, by now, she'd meant to have all the furniture in the baby's room shut up tight so Jared wouldn't see it. When the delivery had been delayed, she hadn't had a phone number for him to put off his coming over.

But her secret was popping out in the shape of her belly, anyway. She knew she'd been lucky it'd happened later rather than sooner in her pregnancy because she'd been dreading having to face the questions.

Why not start with explaining her pregnancy story to Jared? He was the closest thing she had to a friend in town, which was sad. But it'd been her decision to stay private. She still talked to all her old friends—the ones who *hadn't* slept with Brett—on the disposable cell phones she bought. She never told them where she'd gone or that she was pregnant, although she assured them she was happy and safe.

Privacy, she thought. And discretion. She didn't want to do anything to raise a red flag and encourage Brett to find her.

"So," she said, crossing her arms in front of her chest. She was wearing a baggy sweater, but she still felt as if every pregnant part of her—from her buxom boobs to her belly—was on display. She'd also read that most women started feeling unattractive once they hit their third trimester, but…well, she'd liked the bigger boobs. And she liked the roundness of her belly, too. "I guess the cat's out of the bag."

He stuck his hands in his jeans pockets, and that's when she knew for certain that he'd already guessed she was pregnant.

"Not to be fresh, but your cat's becoming pretty obvious," he said.

"How many people do you think have noticed?"

"I have no idea. But it was just the other day when I thought I saw..." He made a slight curving motion with his hand in front of his belly.

"Ah." A flush steamed up her face. Either the good people of St. Valentine hadn't been looking very hard at her or Jared had been...

Well, looking more than anyone.

She almost fanned herself at the very thought. It was nice to be looked at by him, even though she wanted to discourage it.

"Pardon me for asking," he said, "but why do you care if everyone finds out?"

Oh, goody, here it went. The big-league lies.

The words rushed out. "I was seeing the baby's father when I got pregnant, but he passed away before he ever knew." Liar. "I came here to start over."

That was definitely the truth.

Even so, Jared was frowning, as if she'd tripped up in her story already and he'd caught onto the snag.

Did the man have a built-in BS detector or something?

He surprised her by circling around the hundred other questions he could've asked, but she could tell the subject was still on his mind.

"It looked as if some of that baby stuff needs assembly," he said.

"I thought I'd take care of that today while you were

in the backyard. I want to start arranging the baby's room before it gets too hard to move around at all."

"I've got time enough to help out."

But he didn't move. Instead, he peered around her condo, as if taking in the details that she was so reluctant to give out to anyone.

What did he see in the sparse furnishings, like the sofa and the curtains she'd bought at a second-hand store in New Town? Or the retro pop prints—the Andy Warhol–inspired panel art featuring old-school starlets—she'd seen in a boutique window and which were now hanging on her walls?

Actually she had splurged on those because she hadn't been able to afford much after leaving the wedding. She'd cut up her credit cards early on, avoiding a paper trail. All she'd been able to do when she'd left Brett was make a quick trip to the bank and empty what she had in her account, which had been meager at best.

Yes, money had always been modest in the Olsen household.

Until she'd met Brett and fallen for him.

Without waiting for Annette to give the go-ahead, Jared brazenly went for the baby's room, his boot steps heavy on the carpet.

His take-charge attitude sent that thrill through her again, but she banished it. Brett had been a real I'll-take-care-of-this guy, too, and with every footstep she heard, the reminder was stamped into her.

She followed Jared into the second bedroom, which showed hints of the baby who would make this place into a real home in a short time. A Thumper wall hanging was the first decoration she'd purchased out of her initial waitressing paycheck, and she'd bought something small each time afterward: a mobile that was sitting in the corner and waiting for a crib to dangle over, a pile of soft blankets, a rocking chair she'd found at a yard sale a month ago. She'd finally had enough money to get the real big stuff just last week, and she planned to buy even more when she could afford to after putting aside a chunk of funds for medical bills and maternity leave.

Jared was standing in the midst of the baby paraphernalia, completely out of place, just like Gulliver in Lilliput.

He pointed to a box. "It says *bathinette*. Did they misspell it?"

"No." She held back a smile. "You're thinking of a bassinet. I have one in my room since the baby will be in there at first. A bathinette is a combination of a bath and a changing station."

"I see."

Now he seemed even more uncomfortable, and she would've merely chalked it up to him being an alpha male who couldn't stand the notion of diapering a baby…except for that dark shadow that seemed to cover him every once in a while.

He went over to a storage unit and ran his hand over the smooth birch wood. "So this baby of yours…do you know what it is?"

"It?"

He still wasn't looking at her.

She frowned. "I don't know the sex yet. I wanted to be surprised at the birth, but…"

That's when he finally met her gaze, and what she saw ripped into her. A sense of understanding?

Just what was going through his mind?

His voice was hoarse when he said, "But you're starting to wonder now. Boy or girl. You're starting to look at the little outfits in the stores and think, 'Should I buy this in blue or pink?'"

"If I didn't know any better, I'd say you know something about that, Jared."

He froze, then gathered himself and knelt in front of the bathinette box. "I don't know a thing about what it's like to have a child."

The words hovered like a thick mist near the ceiling but never descended.

Instead, he began to read the directions on the box. Then he opened it, as if that looming reminder of what he'd just said wasn't even there. "This one is easy enough. It just folds open."

As she watched, he got it ready. It took mere minutes.

When he was done, Annette's hand went to her chest. She could just see her boy or girl on top of the changing station, smiling up at her, waving tiny hands and feet, gurgling and looking at her as if she was the only person who mattered in the world.

Strangely enough, when she glanced at Jared, he was staring at the top of the bathinette, too, as if he was seeing a child.

But he brusquely turned away from it. "You said there's a bassinet?"

"In my room. That'll take some assembly, though."

"I've got it. Do you have tools?"

She was almost embarrassed to get her silly little kit for him, but it had screwdrivers and a hammer and wrenches and the most basic single-girl items she might need in a rented condo where she could just call the owner—her manager at the diner—for some help. Even so, she knew how to use what she had.

When she returned, he'd left the baby's room and gone into her master bedroom, with its equally Spartan decorations: more pop art on the walls, a single dresser and a wicker trunk at the foot of her twin bed.

In an oddly intimate moment, she swallowed at the sight of him standing near the mattress.

Big enough for only one, she thought, unless she wanted a really cozy night with someone.

Like Jared?

She handed over the kit, stepping away from him just as fast as she could. "Clearly I won't be building a cabinet or anything in the near future, but these tools should do."

"They're just fine." He grinned at her, taking her breath away. Without his hat, he didn't resemble the Black Bart he seemed to want to be every time he walked into a building in St. Valentine. He seemed less like a badass legend in the making and more like a man who would help out a woman anytime she needed it.

As he extracted the parts from the box, she felt as useless as a bike without wheels.

She pointed to the door. "I'm just going to…"

Finally, he seemed to register the results of that BS test that had obviously been running through his brain this whole time, ever since she'd lied to him about how she'd gotten pregnant. "You know that you don't have much of a poker face."

"What do you mean?"

"Annette…" He seemed to have trouble getting past the sound of her name. It was the first time he'd ever used it with her.

She liked hearing it, though. Probably too much.

He tried again. "When you were telling me about the father of your baby, you got this…expression. As if you didn't think I'd believe what you were spinning."

Seriously? Sure, she'd had to create a bit of a story when she'd been hired on at the diner, but it had worked then. She'd even seemed trustworthy enough to Terry, the manager, that after about two weeks, she'd moved out of the St. Valentine Hotel and into this condo that he owned, paying cash on the barrel to rent it.

Why couldn't she pull the wool over this guy's eyes?

"You want to tell me the real story?" he asked while beginning to put together the bassinet.

"If I told you, would you keep it under wraps? I'm serious about that."

He looked over his shoulder and grinned at her, and she couldn't help but trust him. Then he nodded.

Boy, what he did to her with just a glance…

She inhaled, then dove in, realizing right away that it actually felt good to unload like this. Just as good as Tony Amati had probably felt when he'd written in his journal.

Besides, it seemed she couldn't lie to Jared, anyway, and she needed *someone* here in St. Valentine. Why not him—the man who was putting together her baby furniture, the constant gentleman who sat like a sentinel at the diner counter most days?

"I did have a boyfriend," she said. "Or, rather, a fiancé. It was back in Tulsa."

"A fiancé is pretty serious."

"Oh, I felt serious enough about him." She leaned back against a wall, resting her hands under the curve of her tummy. It felt so reassuring. "But there's way more to this story than that. Before I go on, I should tell you that I was raised in a...certain way. It started after my dad died when I was about ten. Cancer."

Jared stopped working. "I'm sorry to hear that."

"Thanks. It was a long time ago. But everything about it stayed with my mom and me for a long time. She was heartbroken—it was hard for me to see that on her face every day. Also, the medical bills from his illness were astronomical, and even though my parents came from good families, they'd hit some hard times over the years. So my mom and I ended up as what Blanche DuBois might refer to as 'the genteel impoverished.'"

He must've known who Blanche was because he didn't ask. He only went back to work.

"At any rate," she said, "my mom never lost hope that I would find some security for my future. She drove that into me. Pretty old school, isn't it? But I wanted to take care of her, too, and I didn't think much about being a gold digger or whatever you want to call it. I was just a kid back then, and I liked the way boys looked at me when my mom dressed me up and told me how to flatter them. And when I got old enough to date, I liked being taken to nice places. She always told me that I should make the best match possible, and it wasn't until she passed away just before I went off to college on a scholarship that I started thinking about how sketchy her coaching was."

"You got a mind of your own at college."

"I did. My mom was really into art, and among other things, she'd given me an appreciation for it, too. So I majored in art history, maybe to feel close to her more than anything, since her death was still pretty fresh, then decided that I wanted to work with children through the arts." She stopped, and brought her explanation back on topic. "Anyway, I started to date other men—regular guys, some who didn't have a penny to their name. But, what do you know, I finally met someone my mother would've highly approved of."

Much to Annette's surprise, Jared went ahead and fixed the drape canopy over the bassinet—something that she had expected him to save for her. "He was Mr. Right. Right?" he said.

"Ultimately, I came up with a few other choice names for Brett besides 'Mr. Right,' but at that point, I thought that's what he was. The perfect man for me. He was charming, could talk for hours about what we both enjoyed and he was friendly to everyone. His family just happened to be rich, and he was a star athlete. He courted me in a whirlwind, and when he proposed, I said yes."

Jared slowly fixed the ruffled skirt to the bottom of the bassinet. "Then you got pregnant."

He had that tone of voice again—almost as if he was mired in something so deep and thick that he couldn't make his way out of it.

Almost as if, once upon a time, he'd had his heart torn out of him just as thoroughly as hers had been.

As Jared waited for her to answer, he stood and parted the drape canopy of the bassinet. With every piece of baby furniture he'd seen today there came figments of imagination—a little girl in this frilly cradle, in the bath, in the room where Annette's child would soon be coddled by Bambi blankets and with as much love as a mother could give.

But that baby would have only half of a family, just

as he'd made sure his own girl had, before she'd found a whole one with another man.

He'd never seen Melissa in those cute baby outfits with footsies attached to them. He'd never given her a bath. He hadn't even been there when she was born because that had been the role of her new father, and Jared had stayed away, knowing that he wasn't welcome. And knowing that he didn't even deserve any part in her life, after he'd chosen his one true love—the rodeo—over everything else.

So why had he stuck around here today, putting things together for Annette if it was so painful?

The answer was easy: he kind of liked that he knew her secret and that he was even a teeny, helpful part of *this* baby's life, putting together his or her first furniture.

It even made him feel as if, for a fantasy-filled moment that would never materialize, he was a kind of family man who had atoned for his mistakes.

Maybe that's why he'd started tossing questions Annette's way when he'd never done much of that before.

"Didn't your fiancé want the baby?" he asked now as he rested his hand on the rim of the bassinet. "Why would he have married you if he didn't want a family?"

"I never told him about the baby." Annette slid down the wall until she came to the shag carpet, seeming exhausted just at the thought.

Jared wanted to pull her close to him, ease his hand down the hair that she'd worn long today. Even in her khaki pants and loose sweater, she still possessed that higher-class vibe that had struck him much earlier. Now he knew the reason.

If he'd thought she was out of his league before, there

was no denying it now. To think—a rodeo bum and a woman who had an art history degree.

What a pair.

"Why didn't you tell him about the pregnancy?" he asked.

"I was going to. I thought he'd be just as happy as I was, but then…" She shook her head. "I took the pregnancy test right before the wedding ceremony. I hadn't done it before because everything was in such chaos—dress fittings, last-minute details, rehearsal dinners. By the time the big day rolled around, I realized that… Well, I had an idea something was different about me."

He supposed she'd missed her period and was just too much of a lady to say it in front of him.

"Then what happened?" he asked.

"I ignored what everybody always says about keeping the bride and groom away from each other before the ceremony. It's supposed to be bad luck if you see one another at that point, right? But I rushed to his dressing room, anyway." She fidgeted with the edge of her sweater. "He wasn't alone."

Jared tensed up.

Annette noticed. "I see you guessed it. I wasn't the only member of the bridal party who was saying 'I do' that day. And the worst part of it was that she was a friend. A good one, I thought."

"Annette…"

"No, don't be sad for me." She tugged down the sleeves of her sweater, wrapping her hands in them, making her appear more soft and vulnerable. "Something came over me at that moment, just as she was fixing her dress and he was telling her to get out. I knew deep down that I could never love him after that. I felt stupid because I'd never even guessed he'd do something so awful."

"You're not stupid."

"Okay, maybe *ignorant* is the better word because I never had all the information I needed about him. Looking back, I should've known that he was staying out late for more than oil company meetings with his family. Or that he was taking midnight calls in his study from more than business partners. Maybe I didn't want to believe anything was wrong and I ignored the details."

Jared couldn't believe any man could be so idiotic as to play a woman like Annette. But maybe Casey, his ex-wife's husband, had thought something similar about him.

Annette said, "I called the wedding off then and there. Turns out that Brett didn't have the same conclusion in mind."

"He wanted to go through with it, even after that?"

"Yes. He actually tried to justify himself. He told me that his father had been doing it for years and his mom didn't seem to mind. 'Everyone does it,' he said. It was all very Kennedy-esque." She laughed shortly. "Then there was the topper—he tried to apologize for me seeing him in the act."

It struck Jared that she had a maturity that went beyond her years. Maybe that came with the class she carried, even in a small-town waitressing uniform.

"I imagine," Jared said, "that you put him in his place."

"I did." Her face went pink, but she didn't add any more.

Something about her reaction made a protective streak flash through him, but when she got to her feet before he could go over to help her up, he realized that Annette didn't need any help from anyone.

And that was fine by him, seeing as how knowing this much about her lent him a sense of responsibility that hadn't been there before. It was a strange feeling for a man who'd never wanted any of it in his life.

She strolled over to the bassinet, just as if she hadn't revealed anything about herself to him. "You did a great job. Thank you so much for everything."

"It was nothing." But that wasn't true. This afternoon had been something.

When she smiled up at him, it was as if his bones turned to hot water, which was apt considering that, if he got too much deeper into her, that's what he'd be in.

Hot, scalding, bubbling water that was likely to strip him bare.

"You have that journal with you?" she asked.

"It's in my coat pocket."

"Mind if I read it while you see to the garden?"

"Not at all." He absently stroked the whiskers on his chin. "There's something I was going to mention about that garden, though."

"What?"

"I'm afraid I'll make a mess of it."

She widened her gaze. "How much of a mess?"

"A mess that might have me repotting and replanting."

She didn't answer for a moment, and he saw his chances at finding any more Tony Amati relics circling a drain. He even wondered if he should start knocking on her neighbors' doors to see if they wouldn't mind a stranger making a disaster zone out of their own backyards.

But a second later, she was smiling at him again. "Your peace of mind is far more important than some herbs. Dig away."

Jared never tolerated big shows of emotion, but he definitely felt a victorious inner fist pump inside of him now.

"Great. Thanks, Annette." He had the grace to seem sheepish. "Truth is, I have pots and tools from Gran's in the back of my truck already."

Her eyes sparkled, just as they did when they were in the diner across the counter from each other. But this time, there was no barrier between them, and his heart started doing a panicked, stimulated dance.

"You can predict what I'll do that easily?" she asked.

He managed a small laugh because she was leaning closer to him.

And when she was just inches from him, he thought—no, he wished—that she would stand on her toes to plant a kiss on his cheek. The very idea seemed to shine in her eyes.

Or maybe that's just what he wanted to see there.

His pulse seemed to fill the slight space between them.

Bang, bang. Each sound echoed against her, then right back at him, hitting him hard in the chest, the belly.

But then she blinked, as if she were coming out of a spell, and he did, too, barring his chest with his arms out of a lack of any better response.

She laughed, cutting the tension, and started to walk out of the room. But then she turned back, her voice a bare, nearly shaking whisper, as if she'd suddenly realized that she shouldn't have told him a thing about herself.

"Jared, Brett doesn't know where I am."

That protective streak reared up again. Good God. She'd run away from Brett?

She was watching him closely. "You're going to keep my secret, just like I'll keep the one about Tony's journal, right? Because I'm going to have to lie to the rest of this town. I don't want Brett to ever find me."

That vulnerability he'd only now discovered in her clutched at his rarely used heart, and he couldn't help giving himself over to her, just this once.

His voice was as quiet as hers when he said, "I won't say a word."

Chapter Four

As the clouds parted to reveal a splash of afternoon sun, Jared tipped back his hat and got to his haunches, surveying the garden.

And the mess.

He'd started near the white picket fence, which lined the little concrete patio and herb-spotted patch of dirt that Annette called a backyard. It'd been obvious where she'd been digging when she'd come upon the journal—almost right up against the fence itself, near a dying butterfly bush that she'd told Jared she wanted to take out. It seemed that, when the fence had been put in, the workers had just missed hitting Tony's journal with the posts.

So Jared had started there.

Yup, he'd been honest with Annette when he'd said he was going to do some damage, far more honest than he'd been a couple of hours ago, when he'd told her, *I don't know a thing about what it's like to have a child.*

All the time he'd been working, the lie had stabbed at him. But why should he feel compelled to spill his guts to her just because she'd done it for him when she'd talked about her ex-fiancé?

Maybe it was because, even now, years after Jared had left his daughter behind, the guilt still weighed heavy on him. Could that be the reason a part of him wished he could unburden himself to someone?

He wouldn't do it, though. Couldn't. Especially to Annette because he couldn't stand to think of the look she'd probably give him if she found out that he was just as immoral a man as her ex-fiancé had been in a lot of basic ways.

Behind him, the screen door slid open. He didn't have to turn around to know Annette was there because he could feel her presence, tickling his back like the soft touch of fingers over skin.

"Hungry yet?" she asked.

He brushed off all the heaviness that'd been perched on his shoulders. "You planning on rewarding me with food for tearing up your backyard?"

She laughed. "After you taste my food, I'm not sure you'll be calling it a reward."

He finally looked over his shoulder. She was still wearing that simple white baggy sweater over khaki pants, but it was enough to send his libido pumping. It seemed that all she had to do to turn him on was appear.

And if that wasn't a dangerous thing, he didn't know what was.

Standing, he brushed off his jeans with his glove-covered hands. "I'm sure your cooking is good."

"I'm no Top Chef, but I'm no bottom one, either. Why don't you just take a break and see for yourself?"

Smiling, she stood aside as he stripped off the gloves, dropped them to the patio, then moseyed toward her and the condo. While he wiped his boots on a fake-grass mat with a plastic daisy blooming in the corner, he tried not to let the smell of her hair get to him. Was it lilies?

Once inside, the aroma of her meal took over, and he went to the washroom, taking care not to make an even bigger mess than he already had outside as he soaped off the dirt and got himself halfway presentable. He even doffed his Resistol, hanging the hat on a hook on the back of the bathroom door, for lack of a better idea.

Just before he left, he caught sight of himself in the mirror, and he quashed the urge to run his fingers through his dark hair to wrangle it into some kind of style.

But why take those sorts of pains? It wasn't as if he should be impressing Annette Olsen.

He went to the quaint kitchen, with its cheery yellow curtains and a few knick-knacks on the counter—a farmhouse napkin holder, a wooden block holding a set of knives, a few cookbooks piled on each other, all of them with healthy titles like *Mommy's Organic Kitchen.*

Annette noticed the direction of his gaze as she pulled out a cushioned chair for him at the tiny, age-scratched pine table. "Don't worry. I didn't put stuff like weird cheeses or quinoa in the meal."

"What the hell's keen-wah?"

She laughed again, and it seemed to come so easy to her when, for so many years, he hadn't been able to laugh himself.

But here he was, smiling. "So sue me. I've never heard of the junk."

"To tell you the truth, I didn't even know how to say *quinoa* the first time I read about it in a recipe. I found out that it's what they call a pseudocereal with a lot of protein. Maybe I'll whip some up for you someday."

Someday.

The word balanced on his shoulders, taking the place of the guilt he'd felt earlier. He barely moved, fearing that her offer might fall off him with one false start.

But why should he care if it did?

She brought over a plate with a grilled cheese sandwich, dill pickle slices and some funny-looking multicolored shoestring chips, plus a steaming bowl of soup. She'd already set out the silverware, and he took a red-striped napkin and spread it over his lap, just as if he was in a high-class joint.

And, truthfully, he kind of was, mostly because Annette made it seem that way. She seemed to class up anyplace she was in.

He picked up one of the shoestring things.

"Those would be vegetable chips," she said, sitting down with her own food. "And I have to warn you that they're addictive."

"You think a man can survive on them?" There didn't seem to be much to them.

"If they're too prissy for you, I can run out and get you some greasy, manly onion rings."

He popped the food into his mouth and damned if he didn't like it.

"See?" she said, looking mighty pleased. "Eating healthy isn't going to kill you, but I have to say, I even had to get used to it."

"You had good reason to make a change." He gestured toward her belly, which was hidden by the table.

She rested her hand on her tummy, as if happy that she didn't have to hide her pregnancy anymore. "There're a lot of changes I've made. Meals, exercise, lifestyle."

Before he knew it, he asked, "How far along are you?"

Shut up, Colton, he thought. *There's no need for you to be digging anywhere but in the dirt outside.*

She didn't mind, though. "Third trimester."

"And you still run around the diner?"

She dipped her spoon into the soup. "Technically, I don't run. You might've noticed the changes I've made with work, too. I take breaks and sit down whenever I can. But, soon, I'm going to have to tell Terry about why I'll need some time off."

The diner's manager seemed to be a stand-up guy, based on St. Valentine gossip. Lord knew that Jared had made an art of listening to all the talk going on around him and sorting through it for truths and falsehoods, especially when it came to Tony Amati.

He stirred his soup. Nothing about the manager of the diner or how he accommodated his pregnant waitress would be his affair, but, for the first time in his life, he felt protective of someone. Felt as if he could be something like a friend to Annette before he got his business done in St. Valentine and left it behind.

He hadn't been much of a friend to anybody. Not his wife. Not to the daughter who'd ended up better off without him, anyway. Considering all that, now he started to wonder if it was friendship or all that remaining guilt making him ask questions about Annette and her child.

"What is it?" she asked, munching on a vegetable chip. "Is the soup terrible?"

"No, not at all." He took a spoonful in, just to prove it. "Best I ever had."

She smiled again as she continued to eat. Jared took a bite of his sandwich, and that was good, too, even with whole-wheat bread. Either Annette had a habit of downplaying her kitchen skills, or she truly didn't know that she could cook grilled cheese with the best of them.

Meanwhile, he kept thinking about her and the baby.

After polishing off his sandwich, he found himself talking.

Again.

"Do you ever get nervous about…"

"The future?" She caught on right quick, as if she'd been hoping he would be up for more chatter. "Sure. I'd be a fool not to be concerned about how I'm going to take care of my baby the best I can. I know I'm going to be a great mom, though."

He nodded, his throat tight. He wondered what was so wrong with him that he'd never been so confident about being a good dad. That he had made every choice possible to avoid being one at all.

Like birth mother, like son, he thought.

Clearing his throat, he couldn't help asking, "So you're going to raise him or her all on your own?"

Annette set down her spoon, tilting her head. "Why wouldn't I?"

"You're a single mom with no one to help you out."

"Jared, are you asking if I ever thought about giving this baby up?"

From the expression on her face, he knew that it had never even been something she'd considered. For the first time in his life, a spark of sunlight touched him, right in the center of his chest, but he quickly snuffed it out.

They were so different, Annette and him. One of them was made to be a parent, the other...

Not hardly.

He wolfed down the rest of his food so he wouldn't have to talk anymore, but he could tell that Annette was searching for something to say. Wasn't she perceptive enough to know that there was a line between him and everyone else that shouldn't be crossed?

Even if he'd just done some heavy-duty crossing himself?

Finally, he wiped his mouth with the napkin, stood, then cleared his plate.

"That really hit the spot," he said. "Thanks for going to the trouble."

"No trouble at all, Jared."

It was too much for him—her using his name in a setting that was far more private than the public anonymity of the diner. Not to mention her sitting there with her light blond hair shining under the kitchen light, begging for him to just let down his guard and run a hand over it.

After retrieving his hat, he went back toward the garden, where he wouldn't be tempted.

And where he wouldn't have to stop himself from asking questions that shouldn't concern him.

Annette sat at the table long after Jared excused himself. She couldn't figure him out. In the diner, he was one man—closed off, yes, but open to a little bit of easy banter.

But here?

Here she'd seen another man. More guarded than usual. Seemingly haunted in some way, too. It was as if their time in the baby's room when he'd been putting together that furniture had changed him in some way.

What was his story?

And why was she hell-bent on wondering about it?

Carefully, she rose from her chair, using the back of it to help her up. She'd never had to do that before her recent tummy pop, so she slowed down as she went about cleaning up the kitchen.

Had she said too much today about her life, and had that put off Jared in some way? After all, he'd only come to her place to search the garden for Tony Amati artifacts. It hadn't been as if he'd promised to be her best friend or confidant or a sounding board for all her woes.

So why had she felt as if there was something connecting them earlier, during their baby-room conversation? An understanding. Simpatico.

That was why she still didn't regret confiding in him today, even though she'd stopped short of telling him about Brett's near abuse on their wedding day. It was just that Jared seemed so interested in her story, and in a town of strangers who had no real idea who she was or what she had run from, confiding felt good.

So did his questions about the baby.

Not that she needed a man around to be interested or to help her put together furniture or to eat her grilled cheese. Nope. It was just that knowing someone like him was around was nice.

As she went to the kitchen window, she spotted

Jared, whose cowboy hat was tipped so low that she couldn't see much of his face.

The quiet drifter who'd wandered into her life. He really didn't belong—not at her dinner table and definitely not anywhere near her libido.

Too bad her libido wasn't listening, though. It was burning in the center of her, low and deep, tingling as she watched him bending to a knee in the dirt, his hands encased in those heavy gloves that he probably wore on the Harrison ranch as he mended fences and worked until his muscles strained against his shirt, just as they were doing now.

Blowing out a ragged breath, she rinsed the dishes and wiped down the counters. Then she went to the secondhand faux-leather sofa in the family room, turned on a reading light and sat down.

There'd be no more looking out kitchen windows today. No, sir.

No more mulling over Jared Colton.

Instead, she grabbed Tony Amati's journal, which was waiting for her on the worn leather chest that served as a coffee table.

Leaning back on the sofa, she propped up her feet, opening the book, its brittle pages smelling like an old house.

"Just what are you about, Tony?" she murmured as she started reading.

While she immersed herself in his entries about the much younger woman he loved, she lost track of time.

It is hard to be blind—or to at least attempt it. Because this is how I spend so much of my time when I see her in town, strolling down the board-

*walk, her gaze straight ahead while I pretend not
to see her or the secretive smile she wears while
she pretends she doesn't see me, as well.*

Annette turned the page, imagining the dark-eyed
former Texas Ranger in front of the St. Valentine Hotel
or the old mercantile store, lounging on a bench, smoking a cigar and aching for the woman he loved.

What had she looked like? Was this even the woman
who might've given birth to Tony's child?

*Today, she went into the bridal boutique, and it
was all I could do to keep from going inside to
stop her from trying on the dress she is to wear on
her wedding day to another man. But what would
I have done then? Ridden off with her into the sunset? Taken her someplace where no one knows
our names? I don't want that sort of life for her,
because I know what it is to need a new home,
away from everything you have known before.*

Again, Annette paused. Tony had *needed* a new
home? Was that the reason he'd ended up here, out
West?

Why did it sound as if he hadn't come here out of
choice?

She felt a kinship with him; she'd run away from
the only life she'd known, too, but she'd never heard
that Tony had been fleeing something. In the articles
Violet and Davis Jackson had written about him, he
was known as a man who'd supposedly made his way
to what would eventually become St. Valentine just to
find a better life. He was an American success story.

But, from the way he'd written this, she wasn't so sure about that.

I should have stayed away from her, but I am not so strong. I walked by the boutique window, looking out of the corner of my eye, hoping to see her again...and hoping not to....

Yet there she was, and I nearly broke all my promises to myself about the other night, when we gave in to each other for the first time and vowed to keep it a secret. She was in her dress, reluctantly showing it to her best friend in the world, who held her hand over her heart and smiled in approval. A white dress, just as pure as her sighs whenever we kiss. Just as beautiful as she could have been if life had not made me what I am—a man who is all wrong for her.

The thought of that white dress intrigued Annette's imagination. Once upon a time she had owned one of those, too, and it had also been for the wrong husband. She'd sold it months ago, getting only a fraction of what it was worth, although it had been enough for her to purchase some pots and pans for her new kitchen.

A good trade, even if she said so herself.

But as the image of the dress faded in her mind's eye, her gaze fell on the last words she had read.

A man who is all wrong for her.

From the backyard, the sound of metal hitting dirt intruded on her thoughts.

Jared. Keep-to-himself, secretive, is-he-or-isn't-he-trustworthy Jared.

He was all wrong for her, too, no matter what her sex drive told her with all its revving and purring.

Jeez, when were the hormones going to fade? Then again, she'd read that some pregnant women were hornier than ever at this stage.

Great.

She put down the journal, closing its cover gently, letting her hand linger on it. It was almost as if she didn't want to crush the feelings Tony Amati had written inside.

Then she went to the baby's room to get some work done, shutting the door behind her.

Blocking out the sound of Jared in her backyard.

The minute Jared was off work the next day, he raced the sunset to get to Annette's, knowing that she would be done with her shift by now.

She'd given him the key to the backyard gate yesterday before he'd left, probably because he'd looked so defeated at not having found anything.

"It's too early to give up," she'd said. "Just come back tomorrow, whether I'm here or not."

He'd thanked her, wondering how much deeper he could dig along the fence line before he infringed on her actual garden. He didn't want to start uprooting every single herb, so he decided that, tonight, he would concentrate his effort *outside* the fence because it was still close to where she'd unearthed the journal.

By the time night fell, with the stars shining down on him, he'd turned over a lot of ground outside her picket fence—and he'd attracted some attention from Annette's neighbors, although no one had come out and asked him what he was doing. If they did, he was prepared to give them a story about hearing there were arrowheads out here or what-have-you. For all they knew, it could be a quirky hobby of his.

He stood, leaning on his shovel, surveying all the open land that ran from the condo complex to a playground off yonder.

Was it possible that there were Tony Amati artifacts scattered from here to there instead of inside her property?

He flexed his gloved hands, which had gotten tight, but he was damned if he was going to give up yet.

A voice floated to him in the darkness. "Remember that gopher in *Caddyshack?*"

He hadn't expected to feel like a ten-alarm fire was raging in his gut just at the sound of Annette's voice, but there it was.

He tried not to show how she affected him as he stripped off his gloves and tucked them into his back jeans pocket. "What about gophers?"

Handing him a big ceramic mug with steam curling from it, she said, "The one in that movie wasn't your ordinary digger. He was pretty much the superhero of gophers. You could've given him a run for his money, though." She gestured toward the upset earth around them.

"If I had a dime for every hole I've made during the past two days…" he said as the aroma of hot cocoa infiltrated his senses. He hadn't realized until now how good it would taste here in the mild chill of the night. Even if winter was generally kind in this area of Texas, the darkness still had a bite to it tonight.

He propped his shovel against the fence. She blew at her drink, cupping her mug with both hands. She was wearing a long felt coat over her waitress uniform, telling him that she had come straight home from the diner.

"Long shift today?" he asked.

"No. I hung around for a short time after work ended. Violet Jackson came in."

Wonderful. "So the reporter's sniffing around again."

"Sure enough. She and Davis just won't give up on the Amati story. Even getting married during the middle of it all hasn't stopped them from chasing down more leads. I think they'll be on it until they've solved all Tony's mysteries."

"Sorry you're involved with this. They know I eat at the diner, and they think I confide in you about Tony."

It seemed as if she were about to launch into her own investigation about the reasons he was so obsessed with the man, but she held back.

"I'm sure you're right," she said. "But Violet's so nice and casual about chatting me up. Not that I had anything to report to her."

Annette started to walk, and he followed without really even thinking about it. It could've been the stars above. It could've been her perfume.

It could've been anything about her that he couldn't resist, although he damned sure was trying.

"You'd think," he said, "that she and Davis have some sort of sixth sense about things, like she knows you found the journal."

"I doubt it." Annette laughed. "Although…"

"What?"

She took a moment, then shook her head. "I read Tony's journal all the way through after you went home last night. There're some odd things in there, don't you think? Things that might turn any investigation in another direction."

My terrible sins...

As the phrase stayed with Jared, he and Annette arrived at the nearby playground, where the swings stirred in a slight breeze and the slides and monkey bars cast shadows on the ground.

Jared leaned against the swing-set pole, his heart beating faster than usual. He could've sworn that it was loud enough for Annette to hear it.

"You didn't say anything about those 'odd things' to Violet, right?" he asked.

"No."

She gave him a long glance that sent a million pleasant—and forbidden—shivers down his body. Then she sat in one of the swings.

"Why does it matter, Jared?" she asked. "Why don't you want them to know anything about your interest in Tony?"

"Because privacy is a virtue." And it was a necessity for some who liked to remain a stranger. Life was easier that way, never having an opportunity to let anyone else down as he'd done to others.

Annette cocked her head, and her unbound hair spilled over a shoulder, catching the moonlight. He ached at the sight, averting his gaze.

"I just don't get you sometimes," she said softly.

The simple words pierced him, though they probably wouldn't have mattered as much coming from anyone else.

And that was probably why he found himself talking again.

"Maybe Tony tried to keep his life under wraps so

he could start over from a past that didn't sit well with him, and I don't intend to exploit that for public consumption," he said. "Maybe he did things that…"

Shamed him?

She dug her sneaker heels into the dirt, holding on to the swing chain with one hand and her mug with the other. "We all have things that we run from. I know that better than anyone."

He thought of her left-at-the-altar groom and the baby she was hiding from her good ol' cheating ex-fiancé.

Maybe she is *a lot like me, with all this running,* he thought. *Only she doesn't have as many years on her, or as much to feel bad about.*

It'd feel so good to set down for a minute all the mental baggage he was carrying, or to have someone look him in the eye and tell him that, someday, he could start again and make amends, as Tony Amati might've done, based on the cryptic things he'd said in that journal.

He drank from his mug. "We both have 'others' we've left behind. I think the two of us should probably leave things at that."

"Can I just ask who you mean?"

Why would she want to ask? But the mere fact that she did brought out that ray of lightness in him that kept popping up around Annette.

"An ex-wife," he finally said.

He watched her push the swing back a little, and as it eased forward, the chain creaked like a haunted echo. He wondered if the daughter he'd just failed to mention had ever liked swinging.

Annette must've noticed something in the way he was gritting his jaw because she drank her cocoa, silent.

Nearby, the sound of a romantic Louis Armstrong song floated out from one of the condos, and as he glanced there, he saw that Annette's was the only window without lights or decorations to commemorate the upcoming Valentine's Day Festival, which tied in with the town's name and was expected to attract even more tourists.

For some reason, that made him feel hollow because if anyone deserved color in their windows, it was Annette.

She spoke. "Yesterday, in the nursery, when you were putting together the furniture..."

"Yeah?"

"I got the feeling there was something going on there, Jared. Now, if I'm prying, you go ahead and tell me, but if I'm right..."

Hell, he wasn't going to get anything past her. But instead of pouring out his soul, he offered up something to keep her happy.

"I was adopted," he said, "so I guess all the baby stuff made me kind of...soft."

"You mean sentimental?"

If he'd been expecting her to react to him being an unwanted baby, she didn't reward him with dramatics. And he relaxed a little.

"I don't get sentimental," he said, taking another drink.

"Naturally." She smiled.

His chest warmed, but he chalked that up to the cocoa.

"So," she said, "that's why you asked me what I intend to do with my baby. Because you were wondering if I was going to give him or her away like someone did to you?"

Yup, she'd heard the pain in his voice yesterday, and he wanted to curse himself for being so transparent.

He didn't say anything, and she stood from the swing. One step, two. The closer she got to him, the faster his pulse raced, the hotter his skin got.

And it definitely wasn't because of the cocoa.

"Jared," she whispered, "I wouldn't give my baby up for the world, and I imagine your mom and dad felt the same way about you, even though it turned out that they couldn't keep you."

He forced himself not to flinch at that. But there was something about her determination to love her child and to make him feel better about someone loving *him* that got to him.

When he risked a glance at her, she was merely inches away, all soft skin, angelic hair and big blue eyes.

He melted, not knowing how to stop it.

And not knowing how to stop himself from leaning down, a breath away from her, as the stars and moonlight took him over.

Chapter Five

Annette closed her eyes out of pure anticipation and instinct, smelling the heady scent of Jared's skin.

Hay and musk, she thought. Cowboy and all man.

As she held her breath, she didn't stop to think how crazy this was, being here, a heartbeat away from kissing Jared Colton, the town cipher.

She only wanted to give in to this dizzying moment.

When his lips brushed over hers, she groaned at the burst of electricity that ran from head to toe, sizzling in her veins and burning her to the core.

But he didn't do anything more than that.

Was he testing her, seeing if she would shy away? Seeing if he should kiss her again?

Little did he know that Annette hadn't felt this alive in—how long? Years? Ever? Before she could think about her determination to live without any man to complicate her new, improved life, she stood on her tiptoes, seeking his lips before he could entirely pull away.

While pressing her mouth against his, she barely felt herself weakly extending her arm to the side, dumping her hot chocolate mug to the ground. She heard Jared do the same with his, just before he made a low sound in his throat, then cupped her face in his palms, deepening the kiss.

But, in spite of all the passion, it was so innocent. His lips on hers, fitting together perfectly, just like a first kiss should be.

A wave of yearning swept over Annette. Warm and hot at the same time. Good and bad, because she didn't want this to stop here, even though she knew that it should.

Still, there was something about this man that made her want to throw caution to the wind, to forget about how she'd gotten to St. Valentine and why.

To forget that she barely knew a thing about him.

All she really knew was that he tasted like chocolate, that his lips were really soft for a man who usually wore such a hard expression and that she could stay here all night in his arms.

When he drew in a breath then backed away from her, she gripped his wrists before he could pull away entirely.

The music that had been playing in the near distance traced the air with a murmur. Thank God, too, because she didn't know what to say right now. Heck, she didn't even know if she *could* say anything. It seemed too hard to fill her lungs with oxygen again, too hard to think or to string a sentence together.

"Annette..." Jared finally said.

Here it came, she thought. An apology. An "I really shouldn't have done that."

Even if she didn't know him that well, she could predict that much about him.

"Don't you dare say you're sorry." She kept holding on to his wrists, even though his palms were still under her jaw, his thumbs resting on her cheeks and branding her skin.

She sought his gaze, which was shaded by that cowboy hat, and she wished she could just whip the thing off him so she could see what he was really thinking.

But, just like most of the time, he was unreadable.

"If you planned to be so sorry about kissing me," she said, "you wouldn't have done it in the first place."

He lowered his hands. She let him go.

And, just like that, their moment was over, just as if it'd never happened at all.

Where had it gone?

He stuffed his hands into his jeans pockets, gazing toward the condos. "I've been wanting to do that for months now, you know."

"You have?" She couldn't help but smile at him, encouraging him to go on so they could get their moment back.

She already missed it, even though it was probably for the best. Wasn't it?

"But," he said, facing her, "just because I wanted it doesn't mean it was a good idea to actually do something about it."

Her pulse was tripping along at the same crazy speed as it'd been when he'd kissed her; it hadn't slowed a bit.

"It's too bad," he said, "because now we have…this."

"This?"

He motioned to the space between them.

"Oh," she said, repeating his gesture. *"This."*

It was an acknowledgment that they were attracted to each other. It was a wide space that neither of them knew what to do with now that it had become awkwardly apparent.

He was right, though. Just because they had shared a moment didn't mean this very guarded man had let down even an inch of his well-fortified defenses, and it didn't mean that she was all of a sudden equipped to deal with a relationship that had the potential to make her vulnerable again.

"So," she said. "What're we going to do now?"

He didn't say anything for a second. He only bent to pick up their mugs.

It was terribly clear that the two of them had no business kissing each other, even if she was craving another one with every awakened, needful cell of her body.

She laughed a little, just to cut the tension. "It's okay, Jared. I understand that you're not going to be around St. Valentine for the long term. You're here for Tony Amati."

And not for stolen kisses.

He stood directly in front of her, and there she went, holding her breath all over again.

"Now can I tell you I'm sorry?" he asked.

"For being curious?" She grinned up at him. "No, you can't. Because I was wondering just as much as you were, and now we can just get on with being friends."

That last word sounded strange, but it was what it was. A girl could never have too many friends, anyway.

They both started to walk back to her condo, her

heartbeat still humming as if contradicting everything she had just told him.

As if insanely, impossibly hoping he'd kiss her again someday.

It was a night full of misspent dreams for Annette, who kept repeating the kiss over and over again in her head—the initial flare of hormones as her lips had touched Jared's, the giddy afterglow just before reality had set back in for her.

And, the next day, when she reported to the diner for her shift, her head wasn't much clearer. Neither was her heart, which still jumped every time someone came through the door, then sank when she saw that it wasn't Jared.

Luckily, Fridays were generally busy; people cashed their paychecks and started their weekends early by going out to lunch. And because the Valentine's Day Festival was just around the corner, everyone seemed to be in a good mood, wearing red-and-white sweaters and humming along to the romantic music on the stereo.

Annette told herself that all of it just made the time pass more quickly, and as she manned the counter, she wholeheartedly threw herself into the spirit of things.

She cleared some plates from the counter after a couple of customers left, wiping down the Formica until she got to the end, where the "Chess Nerds" were lost in one of their frequent games.

George Manderly and Dexter Lars had their board set up and were stroking their gray beards and hunching on their stools. Annette was filling their coffee mugs for about the third time when George glanced up at her as if he'd forgotten she even existed.

"He lives," she said.

Dexter was still staring at the board as George stretched his wiry, flannel-clad arms. "Got to check in with reality sometime or another."

As she turned to walk away, she noticed George peer at her tummy.

Then she noticed him wrinkle his eyebrows.

Joy. Here it was—the day when somebody in the diner finally said something about the baby bump she couldn't hide anymore.

His gaze traveled back up to hers, and she just smiled.

Dexter said, "What's keeping you, old-timer?"

Then he followed the direction of his partner's flummoxed stare.

Right away, he turned back to George, his voice a growl. "Don't you dare miss a good chance to shut up."

A red-faced George very quickly got back on his game, burning a hole in the chess board with his gaze. Dexter peeked back at Annette, blushing, too, then went back to considering his pieces.

Annette sighed, especially when she realized that everyone else in the general area had gone stone silent, eating their pies and sipping coffee as if all their concentration was required to complete the activities.

All right. To announce the obvious or not to announce? That was Annette's question.

But was her pregnancy really anyone's business?

A cowboy, a woman and a darling little girl with dark curls that matched her mother's left their booth across the diner, then came to the cash register, cutting Annette a break. She greeted them after placing the coffeepot on its burner.

Conn Flannigan and Rita Niles smiled at Annette as Rita's four-year-old daughter, Kristy, peeked over the counter in anticipation. Annette grinned as she reached into the drawer below the register and gave the girl a lollipop.

"Prepared for the weekend?" she asked Conn and Rita after Kristy said thanks.

Conn had his arm casually draped around Rita's shoulders as he handed over their money. "Normally the hotel is light on business this time of year, but we had a rush. Looks like this weekend's going to be fully booked."

Rita, the owner of the historic St. Valentine Hotel, looked at her fiancé. "It's because of the Valentine's Day Festival lights at the Helping Hands Ranch. It was bound to draw a crowd."

Rita rested her hands on her rounded tummy, absently rubbing it while allowing her adoring gaze to linger on Conn. She couldn't seem to keep her eyes off him every time they came in here. He always returned the affection, clearly in love.

"The lights should really be something," Annette said, ringing up the sale.

Kristy was already sucking on her lollipop, staring directly at Annette's tummy. She looked at her mom's rounded stomach, then back at Annette's.

Taking the candy out of her mouth, the little girl said, "You're just like Mommy."

Annette could just about see everyone in the booths nearby going still again, their ears perking up.

Leave it to a child to voice what everyone else had been thinking.

Rita laughed uncomfortably, taking her daughter by

the hand. Conn suddenly focused all his attention on cramming the change Annette had just given to him into his wallet.

Heck, no sense in pretending now that her swollen tummy was invisible.

"You're right," Annette said to Kristy. "I'm going to have a baby, just like your mom is."

Someone at the end of the counter coughed. One of the Chess Nerds.

Rita paused, as if assessing just how mortified Annette might be at having to address this in front of a crowd. But when she saw everything was fine, she smiled again.

"How far along?" she asked, one mom to another.

She might as well get used to answering, just as she'd announced to Jared. "Third trimester." Annette nodded to Rita's baby bump. "You?"

"Nearing the third, but I'm bigger than you are."

It was as if a social bomb had been defused, although Annette saw that the elderly couple in the closest booth—Janet and Philip Bacon, who owned the mercantile—didn't look terribly happy that a single girl was running around St. Valentine pregnant without a dad around.

Kristy wasn't done with her questioning, and she innocently asked, "Where's the daddy?"

Annette bit the bullet. Looked like it was time to set the stage for the bigger lies to come. "The dad was in a car accident before he found out about the baby," she said. "So he never knew."

"Oh." Rita's gaze was sympathetic. "I'm so sorry to hear that."

"Thanks." She touched her belly, feeling like a jerk

for lying, even though it was the safest way for Annette to go. "We're doing just fine, though."

She made sure everyone heard that last part because it was as close to the truth as she was probably going to get with the public. But she didn't have a choice, if she wanted to keep her life private and take no chances that Brett would ever get wind of his runaway bride and the baby.

Both Conn and Rita gave her encouraging smiles. Then Rita said, "If there's anything you need, you just let us know."

"I'll do that." She'd heard some talk around St. Valentine about Rita's past—how her first husband had abandoned her with Kristy and left her for another woman. It would've been a sad tale, too, if Conn hadn't come into Rita's life and swept her into a true love story.

The bell on the door sounded, and Annette's stomach flipped, just as it always did when she looked to see who was coming in.

This time, though, her tummy did about three revolutions at the sight of Jared strolling inside, tilting back his hat when he saw her.

He gave her a slight smile that spun her around even more as he took one of the open seats at the counter.

"Well," Conn said, his arm still around Rita. "Congratulations about the baby. Maybe you and Rita ought to start up some kind of mom group."

"Pregnant and Proud," Rita said with a laugh.

At the counter, Jared slowly turned his gaze to her. Annette offered a slight shrug.

The elderly couple who'd given Annette the stink eye earlier took a good look at Jared at the counter. Mrs. Bacon raised her eyebrow to her husband as they abandoned their booth, leaving money on the table without waiting for the check.

Little Kristy waved to Annette's bump. "Bye, baby!"

Her parents led her out of the diner, waving, and Annette went back to work, pulling out her order pad and getting her pencil ready while standing in front of Jared.

He was still giving her a surprised stare.

"Cat's out of the bag," she said.

The only other customers remaining at the counter— the Chess Nerds—seemed very determined not to look at her or to make it seem as if they were still listening in. It was bad enough that, whenever Jared entered some place in St. Valentine, the room went stock-still. Now she'd only added fuel to the gossip fire with her own drama.

Jared sat there for a moment longer, then seemed to come to some sort of decision. "If the cat's out of the bag," he said, getting up from his stool, "then it's time for some adjustments."

She had no idea what he was up to when he grabbed an empty stool and slipped behind the counter with it.

"Hey—" she said.

He guided her to sit, then went back to his stool as if he'd done nothing out of the ordinary.

One of the Chess Nerds chuckled. Probably George.

Jared scanned the menu in front of him as Annette just sat and stared.

At that moment, both of the other waitresses on shift—Corie, a redhead with long braids, and Liza, a short-haired brunette—moseyed out of the kitchen with full trays. They'd been putting together salads for a party of ten in the back room.

They both took brief note of Annette on her stool before George chimed in.

"Now don't be yelling at Annette for slacking. She's preggers."

Liza looked back over her shoulder as she passed. "No duh."

Corie followed her. "We thought it'd be rude to just come out and say something about it."

Both women turned the corner by the pie display as Jared slid his menu away from him.

"I'll have the usual," he said, just as if everything were the same as it ever was.

And as if he'd forgotten all about that kiss they'd shared last night. It was as if the man defined the word *cool.*

Annette had it up to *here* with the cool. "You think you've got the right to be sitting me down on stools whenever you please?"

He leaned his elbows on the counter. "The cat's out of the bag now, so why not? It was probably time for you to rest anyway."

"I know how to take care of myself," she said. She didn't tell him about the support hose she'd taken to wearing at work or the bland Large-Marge bras she'd just purchased at the nearest superstore. Both were rather embarrassing but necessary, and she had it all under control.

Next to Jared, Dexter Lars muttered, "He's not the only one who'll be keeping an eye on you here. Get used to it."

George Manderly grunted in agreement.

"See?" Jared said. "I'm not the only one."

Corie returned to the kitchen window, where Declan

had set out one of her orders. She flipped a braid over her shoulder and grabbed the plates, talking to Annette at the same time.

"You're lucky you're about to get off shift. We're gonna get slammed tonight."

"Then *you're* lucky you've got two more waitresses coming in," Annette said.

"What's going on?" Jared asked.

Dexter didn't look away from the chess board as he answered, setting some kind of record for the amount of words he'd ever, in all these months, addressed to Jared.

"The Valentine's Day Festival lights are going on," he said. "That's what's happening."

As Corie brushed by, carrying her plates, she added, "The Chamber of Commerce set up some kind of internet broadcast for it."

"Why?" Jared asked.

Annette couldn't believe he was actually interacting with others. Interesting times. "Davis Jackson set up a bunch of elaborate light displays out at the Helping Hands charity ranch on the outskirts of town," she explained. "Get it? St. Valentine? Valentine's Day? They thought they'd tie the two together."

"Got it."

"It's a sort of warm-up for that big Cowboy Festival they're planning for March. You'll be able to see the light designs from high above, and the chamber of commerce thought the novelty of that would stir up some publicity for the town."

George added, "Davis hired an airplane to film it."

"Ah," Jared said, and that was that.

But why should he be all that excited when he had no future in this town?

Annette tried not to let that bother her, but it did. Imagining a day without him at the diner counter or even in her backyard just seemed…

Empty.

George Manderly continued his run of chatter. "Times, they are a-changin'. Just this summer St. Val's was down in the dumps, and come March…"

Dexter finished for him. "It could be just as if the mine closure never made a ding on us."

He moved his queen. "Checkmate."

"Checkmate, my a—" George cut himself off, then let out a curse.

All the while, Jared remained silent.

But there was a small grin on his face for some reason. As usual, though, Annette had no idea why it was there.

Not until she got off work.

After putting in a short day at the Harrison ranch, Jared had stopped by Annette's condo for only the briefest of time before he'd gone to the Orbit Diner for some grub.

And, as soon as he'd walked in and seen her, all his senses had scrambled.

The kiss. The feel of her skin against his.

He hadn't been able to get any of it out of his head. The memories had stuck with him all night and day, and seeing her again had just made the urge to hold her that much worse.

There was no denying it—Annette got to him like no other woman had before. He'd been young and green when he'd gotten married all those years ago, and he'd also been reeling from a storm of personal revelations about being adopted and unwanted to boot.

And then there'd been the buckle bunnies on the rodeo circuit. No comparison there, for certain.

Annette just burrowed deep into him, into places he'd kept everyone else out of. Jared didn't know if that scared him or made him feel something else entirely that he couldn't identify.

But there he'd sat at the counter of the diner anyway, as if he couldn't stay away.

When she got off work that night, he couldn't help testing his boundaries then, either, speaking before he'd fully thought out just what he was doing.

"Big plans for the night?" he asked, rising from his stool as she came out from the back room of the diner, where she'd grabbed her long felt coat and purse.

"Nothing more than being a homebody," she said.

He'd already paid his bill, so he followed her out the door. But when she started to head toward her old cherry-red Pontiac GTO in the parking lot, he snagged her coat.

She looked up at him, wide-eyed. Was she wondering if he meant to pull her into his arms again?

As much as he ached to do that, he knew he shouldn't. But he didn't want to let her go, either.

"It's not like there's anything on TV to watch," he said. "Why head home?"

"What else do you have in mind for me?" She laughed. "Since you've started running my life and all."

"I only had you sit on a stool."

Something passed over her blue gaze, and he couldn't translate it. Whatever it was, though, was gentle. Maybe even as full of yearning as what he felt whenever he was near her.

"Come on," he said, guiding her toward his pickup.

"If you're coming over to dig, we can just take our own cars."

"I'm putting off the digging for now."

He hadn't known just what he had planned until he'd said it right then, but she went along with it anyway.

After he helped her into his truck cab and took off on Amati Street, then turned on the road leading out of St. Valentine, he drove to a place he'd checked out a few times before.

Annette seemed to know where they were as the pickup climbed uphill, then slowed near a thick bunch of pines at the top. A few other cars were parked around the area, so he steered clear of them.

"Lookout Point, right?" she asked.

"Some people also call it Heartbreak Hill." He backed the truck up so that the rear was facing a view of St. Valentine beneath them, with its lights glowing in the falling darkness. Then he cut the engine. "You know what they say about this place?"

"Sure. There was a man and a woman who fell in love way back during the thirties, and they used to meet here in secret. He wanted to make good out West, and she was a party girl who neglected to tell him about her husband. But he found the two of them in the St. Valentine Hotel and put an end to their affair. Now they're ghosts that haunt the place."

"That's one story about Heartbreak Hill."

She pulled her coat around her. "I also heard that Tony Amati would come up here before the town was even built. He used to sit here and make plans for the future."

And, Jared thought, he probably even used to pine away for the woman he loved after he'd founded St. Valentine.

He checked his watch, then got out of the truck, reaching behind the seat to pull out some blankets. Afterward, he went around to the other side and opened Annette's door.

He offered his hand.

"You have an agenda," she said.

"The lights are supposed to come on soon, right? This is a better place to see them than the internet."

She took his hand, and he helped her out. But when she was standing on the ground, he was slow to remove his fingers from hers. Even when he did, he still felt her skin on his.

"Let's go," he said, thinking he should remove as much of himself as he could from her.

At the rear of the truck he flipped open the tailgate and set down a blanket for a cushion. Then, as carefully as he'd ever done anything in his life, he lifted her, bringing her up to the truck, seating her.

She watched him, her gaze wide again, as he wrapped her in the other blanket.

His face was inches from hers, and it was all he could do to keep from kissing her once more. He even stopped breathing, tried to stop his heart from pounding as loudly as it was.

Fortunately, in the end, he managed to restrain himself, and he climbed up next to her.

As the truck bounced and creaked under his weight, he attempted not to look at her under the moonlight, because, Lord knew, that was what had done him in last night. Moonlight, beautiful long blond hair and eyes like an eternal summer even during winter.

"You bundled me up pretty good here," she said from the depths of her blanket. "It's not that cold in these parts, you know."

"Better safe than sorry," he said.

Or was it better sorry than safe?

For a laden second, they looked at the town beneath them. Just when he couldn't stand it anymore, he spoke.

"My grandma said that Tony's buried somewhere around here."

Annette's voice sounded as if it had been put through an emotional strainer, as if she were just as wracked with tension as he was. "You remember the part in his journal…"

"Where he wrote that he wanted to be buried next to her?"

It had come at the end, just before the pages had abruptly stopped, as if Tony had lost hope or run out of time for some reason.

Annette's voice barely carried over the night. "Do you think she's up here, too, then?"

Jared frowned. If his great-grandmother Tessa were the woman in the journal, as he strongly suspected, then he knew that her ashes had been spread somewhere else—he wasn't sure where. Gran hadn't elaborated when they'd talked family history in the past.

But he said, "I hope she's close to him. As far we know, Tony couldn't have her in life, but maybe he could be near her in death."

Annette glanced at him. "Well, just listen to you."

He pointed to himself. *Me?*

She smiled at his surprised look. "Yes, you. Jared Colton, the closet romantic."

He pulled down the brim of his hat, not knowing what else to do. "I wouldn't say that."

"I would. It's good to know."

He made a sound of denial, but she kept on him.

"You might dress like a bad guy, all in black, but you know what?" She leaned a little closer. "You belong in a white hat."

Her words had obviously been meant to make him feel good, but how could he when he'd done nothing to earn a silver star in his life?

Even worse, he couldn't stand to think about the expression a dedicated mother like her would undoubtedly get on her face if she ever found out that he'd turned his back on his child, leaving her for another man to raise.

Annette kept watching him. "I should know the difference between a white hat and a black one."

"Because of your fiancé."

"That's right."

Now it was as if she was the one who didn't want to talk any more about it. The way she'd said it niggled at him, as if there were more to her story than she'd revealed the other day.

But Annette didn't seem to be one to dwell on the negative, and when the red-and-white lights flashed on down below just to the left of St. Valentine, she sucked in a breath, her face as radiant as the lights that formed huge hearts, cupids in flight and a cowgirl roping in a cowboy, intent on a kiss.

Transfixed, he watched her instead of the light show.

"Have you ever seen anything like it?" she asked, her

smile all-encompassing, one hand covering her heart as her blanket slumped down.

Jared's chest clenched.

No, he'd never seen anything like this, and he wasn't sure how he was going to be able to stand it when it came time to leave her behind, just as he did with everyone else.

Chapter Six

When Jared dropped Annette off at her car in the Orbit Diner's parking lot, she expected him to follow her to the condo, where he could take up where he'd left off with his digging, even if it was dark out now.

Instead, he said, "I guess I'll see you tomorrow."

"You're not coming over?"

"Not tonight."

Then he took her by the hand and helped her out of his truck, just as if she were some kind of grand lady emerging from a limo.

How did he have the ability to make her feel like a million dollars, even if she'd just been riding in a pickup while wearing her waitress uniform? Even Brett, who'd taken her out to five-star restaurants and bought her designer dresses, hadn't made her feel this way.

Then again, her ex-fiancé didn't seem to know how

to treat a woman with sweetness or, more important, respect. If he had, he would've never fooled around with anyone else, and he definitely wouldn't have made jaw-dropping excuses about it afterward.

Jared walked her to her car and she opened the door. It stood between them like a barrier that she wanted to erase.

"Thanks again," she said. "You were right. The Valentine lights were far more entertaining than some TV program."

This man of few words tipped his hat to her, backing away. "Sleep tight, Annie."

She blinked. Annie. It was the first time he'd called her that, and it made her sound like an entirely different person. It felt right to be called something simple and pretty like Annie.

"Night, Jared," she said quietly, easing into her car, smiling to herself.

After he got into his truck, she could tell that he was waiting for her to start her engine, then he could see that she was safely headed home.

A white hat, she thought. A good guy, even though he had seemed discomfited when she'd mentioned it to him earlier.

Again, she wondered why. But there were a thousand things she wondered about Jared, and that didn't mean she would ever find an answer to any of her questions.

She drove home, seeing his headlights in her rear-view mirror, although she knew that the cabin he rented near the Harrison ranch was in the opposite direction. When she pulled into her complex, he went on his way, and she suddenly felt as if something had been taken from her.

Something—someone—she'd gotten all too used to.

After parking in her garage, she went inside, shrugging off her coat and hanging it in the entry closet, the day finally catching up with her. For the first time, she noticed an ache at the small of her back, and she rubbed it. That, plus an itching sensation on her belly, dampened her mood.

Reality had set in again now that Jared wasn't here—aches and pains that she never seemed to notice when he was around.

She blew out a breath, going to the kitchen, thinking she would prepare warm milk with cinnamon and honey before putting some cocoa-and-shea-butter lotion on the dry and stretched skin of her tummy.

But then she peered through her back window.

She couldn't move for a suspended instant, couldn't believe what she was seeing.

Strings of lights on her picket fence, glowing like a necklace of red and white beads.

She went to the sliding patio door, opened it and stepped outside, running her hands over her arms in the night's coolness.

Nope, she hadn't been imagining things—there *were* colored bulbs on the fence, plus white heart-shaped lights hanging off her roof and...

She bit her lip. There was a big red box near the sliding door, decorated with a white ribbon.

Laughing, Annette bent down to open it and found that it was filled with sparkly heart confetti. A box of chocolates was nestled in the midst of it all.

No one could've done this but Jared. He'd probably noticed that her rented condo had been the only one that hadn't been trussed up for the festival. She'd spent money on baby clothes and furniture and just hadn't had the cash for a display of town spirit.

Not until he'd given her so much of it.

A smile quavered as she thought of how her mom had always gone all out for any holiday. Annette had told herself that, this year, she wouldn't be sad when Mom's birthday rolled around in a few days.

She turned off the lights for the time being, then went back into the condo, still glowing from the inside out. And after she'd gotten her warm milk, coated the skin of her tummy with lotion and reclined in bed to rest her back, she grabbed Tony Amati's journal off her night-stand, thumbing to a certain passage that had spoken to her more than any other.

What it is about her that makes my life new? Is it the way she tells me that, no matter what happened in the past, it doesn't matter? Is it the way she makes me actually believe this, even though, coming from anyone else, it would sound like a platitude? She does not know what brought me to St. Valentine yet. I will tell her soon, because if I live a lie with her, I wouldn't be the man she thinks I am, and I love her too much to be less than she deserves.

I could never pretend to be anyone else with her.

Every day, it is an effort to be worthy of her love. But I have already come to peace with the truth that love is pain. Love is work. But love has also given me this new life and new purpose, and there is nothing I would not do to have her love.

Annette only wished she could ask Tony Amati when he'd found this complicated emotion within himself.

And when he'd finally been able to admit that it was real.

Jared was just shucking off his work gloves and coming out of the stables at the Harrison ranch after mucking out some stalls when a fellow hand, Dale Wesley, moseyed up to him.

"Off and running?" the cowboy said, waggling his thick eyebrows.

"My day here is done besides some business that I need to see to at the feed store."

Dale, who couldn't have been more than twenty-five, had a rakish side-swipe grin that charmed a lot of the females in town. Jared had seen proof of that while hanging around the Queen of Hearts Saloon, sitting in the corner and nursing a beer by himself as his coworker kicked up his boots and flirted with the women.

But that easygoing grin faded now. "Just thought you should know, Jared, there's some talk going around."

"Isn't there always?"

"Sure, but it's never been so much about you and Annette before."

Jared bristled. "What do you mean?"

"Listen, I wasn't the one who started any rumors." Dale nudged back his Stetson, revealing a thatch of brown hair. "People get to talking in this town all the time, and suddenly, they're enthralled with Annette's... condition."

The pieces of this conversation had already locked into place all too quickly. "They're speculating about who the father of her baby is."

"Right. I heard that she told Rita Niles that the father died, but that doesn't stop some busybodies from jumping to more exotic conclusions. People get bored here. They love to elaborate. And you've been spending a lot of time with Annette, and that's obviously lent some spark to a few imaginations."

"Aw, come on." Jared slapped his gloves against his thigh. "Are you telling me somebody's just entertaining themselves with a lie?"

"I guess so, but I'm just the messenger here, pardner."

"Do you know who started this rumor?"

"Pick anyone who might've been in the diner when Annette and Rita were talking."

Jared hadn't paid any attention to the crowd last night. Besides, he'd walked into the conversation late, after he'd been over at Annette's decorating her backyard for the Valentine's Day Festival instead of doing his digging.

"Just thought you should know," Dale said, clapping a hand on Jared's shoulder on his way into the stables.

Jared's temper was the kind that grew with a slow burn, and as he made his way toward his truck, hopped into it, then drove to his cabin to shower and dress into new jeans and a shirt, that temper was at a simmer.

What could he do about the tongue-wagging besides wage his own campaign against the gossip? And how could he track down whoever had started the rumor?

Damn, why did people have to misspend their time by gossiping about everything from him and Annette to him and Tony Amati?

Instead of heading toward Annette's condo and all the digging that awaited him there, he drove to the diner.

He didn't know exactly what he planned to do about this ridiculous rumor, but it might be best to check with Annette to see how she was holding up. Then he could figure out some damage control.

No one was going to make her life any harder than it had to be.

When he poked his head inside the diner, George Manderly and Dexter Lars were at the counter playing chess. It was limbo time between lunch and early dinner, so business was at a lull, and they looked up at the sound of the bell as it filled the room.

"Seen Annette around?" Jared asked.

The elderly men must've recognized some steam rising in Jared, and George pointed to his right, out the long window.

"She's on break," he said.

Dexter added, "She took a walk to the hotel. She likes to sit out front and watch the world go by when Old Lady Ferris isn't camped there smoking her cigars."

Jared had known about Annette's penchant for relaxing on that bench. It was one of those casual things he'd found out early on.

George said, "Just to be clear, we didn't say a word about nothin', Jared."

Both of their grizzled jaws were set, as if they were just as offended by this rumor going around as Jared was.

"Has she already heard what people are saying?" he asked.

"I think so," Dexter said, "but you wouldn't know it."

Jared thanked them and went on his way. Of course Annette wouldn't seem affected by small-town small talk. The actual truth about the father of her baby was far worse than a dumb story about Jared being the dad.

He slowed his steps as he approached Amati Street and the boardwalk. God, had he really just thought that it wasn't a bad thing that some people assumed that *he* was the father?

The very idea was ridiculous, all right, but it also sent another random thought flashing through his head.

Would it actually make Annette and her child's situation better if Jared *did* agree to act as if he were the child's dad? No one could pinpoint exactly when they had met, seeing as both of them had come to town around the same time and no one knew them all that well. And it probably wasn't a stretch to think that he and she had...

He put all thoughts of sex out of his mind. He could handle a lot in life, but he couldn't go there right now.

Yet, on a practical level, he still couldn't let go of the notion that if he didn't deny this new rumor, he would be giving Annette a solid cover story should her ex-fiancé ever get it in his head to track her down. Of course, the story wouldn't beat a paternity test if Brett demanded one, but maybe her ex wouldn't have the desire to request it if Jared were around to actively discourage him.

If he were around...

His boots thudded on the planked walk as he made his way past the busy Queen of Hearts Saloon, toward the Old West–tinged St. Valentine Hotel. As he drew closer, he didn't see Annette out front by the bench, which was occupied by some scruffy guys he recognized as ex-miners. And they weren't the type of ex-miners who had come around to recently making their peace with the rest of the town years after the mine had been shut down by the Feds because of a safety exposé that Davis Jackson had written and published. They were the type who still clung to their bitterness, feeling forced out of St. Valentine when they'd had to claim jobs in the natural-gas fields out near Houston.

Looked as if they were home for the festival, and when they laid eyes on Jared, they were already wearing dirty-minded grins.

Jared's temper had been just simmering before, but he felt his blood rolling and popping now.

As he walked past them, willing to ignore their suggestive looks, one of the ex-miners tugged down on the brim of his baseball cap and muttered to his buddy, "If it ain't the lucky hombre who got it in to Blondie."

Even in a fit of temper, Jared had never been one to go overboard, and it wasn't any different now. All he did was grab the front of the guy's flannel shirt, twisting it as he brought him up against the old wood of the hotel.

"I'd love to discuss this when my front's to you instead of my back," Jared said through his teeth.

Baseball Hat smiled, then moved his gaze to his left.

When Jared saw Annette standing there, her hand to her throat, her mouth agape, he let go of the ex-miner.

The guy laughed and went back to his friends as Annette turned around and quickly walked away.

"Annie—"

Catcalls came from behind him, but he didn't pay them any mind. Not with the look he'd just seen on Annette's face.

There'd been a sort of horror there, and Jared couldn't reconcile that to a face that was always smiling.

"Annie!" he said, finally catching up to her by an alley that lined the side of the Queen of Hearts.

He guided her into it, and she raised her hands, palms out, as if warding him off.

He stopped in his tracks.

She had her eyes closed, as if she couldn't stand to look at him, and it was like a blow to his gut. He'd been expecting this kind of reaction from her if she ever found out about the daughter he'd left. But now?

Now he didn't know what to do but stand there helplessly.

Finally, he found his tongue. "They said something that I wasn't about to countenance, Annie. It wasn't my best moment, but—"

"Stop." She had her back to the wall, her hand on her stomach now.

"Are you okay?" he asked, panic forcing him forward.

"Yes, Jared, I'm fine. The baby's fine."

"Thank God." He bunched his hands at his sides. "I wasn't picking on that guy for no reason, you know."

"I heard what he said, Jared."

"Supposedly people are saying stuff like that all over town, and it isn't right."

"That's not why I…." She shook her head. "I'm sorry. I just saw you there, getting in his face, and it reminded me of…"

Something far deeper than what it seemed was happening. Jared thought about what she'd said to him last night about how she was pretty good at knowing when a man should wear a white hat instead of a black one.

He lowered his voice. "What's going on?"

There was a chair by the back door to the saloon, and he led her to it, sitting her down. She pulled her coat around herself.

"That day when I caught Brett with a bridesmaid," she said, "things didn't go as smoothly as I described when I called him out on it."

He tensed up. "What do you mean?"

"I mean that he didn't like how I was 'sassing' him, and he raised his hand to me."

The remnants of Jared's temper shot up, gathering in his head, nearly blinding him.

"But," Annette said, obviously seeing how his face had gone ruddy and his hands had fisted again, "that's why I didn't stick around. That's why I took off in my car and never looked back. I wasn't about to give him a second chance, because he showed me everything I needed to know about him. Men like that don't change, and when I saw you and that ex-miner..."

"I would never lay my hands on you like that, Annie. *Never.*" He'd done some crappy things, but nothing like that.

Emotions that he'd never felt before—a rage that went beyond mere anger, shock, hurt for what had almost happened to Annette with her fiancé—swamped Jared, bringing him to a knee in front of her.

He took her hand, not bothering to check himself, not bothering to think how Jared Colton didn't reveal himself to anyone.

"Tell me you're not afraid that I'm going to be like that, too," he said, his voice ragged. "Tell me you don't think I'm like Brett."

"No, I don't. It was just that seeing it..." Her grip tightened on his. "It brought back some unpleasant memories."

As he searched her gaze, he saw that, in spite of her

words, she really wasn't sure who Jared Colton sincerely was.

White hat? Or maybe just a really dark gray one.

Hell, he still didn't know which it was, either, even after reading Tony's journal in the hopes that it would tell him what was in his past, his blood.

He wrapped her hand in both of his. "It won't happen again. I swear it."

"I know it won't." She nodded, and the light started to come back into her eyes. "You're tough in so many ways, Jared, but I can't help the gut feeling that being cruel to women isn't one of them."

Oh, he'd been cruel in the past, all right, but it wasn't in an explosive way. Just in a neglectful one.

And he regretted it down to his very core.

Was this his chance to make up for that, though? By protecting Annette and making her life easier while he could?

Tony would've done that, Jared thought, holding on to the only hope he had. *Tony was going to tell the love of his life whatever truths he needed to confess to her. He would've told* me *to do the same and to reshape my life for the woman I...*

As with everything else, Jared didn't have an answer for what Annette had become to him, either.

Jared couldn't put off digging any longer, and when he went to Annette's that evening after he ran some errands in town, he wondered what kind of reception he would get, even though they'd cleared the air.

Would it be back to square one, where they'd started, with her being polite to him and him being polite to her, as if these past few days had never happened?

When he came in through her back gate, he took solace in the fact that, when he'd walked her back to the diner this afternoon, she had seemed fine, although he couldn't stop wondering if he'd planted a seed of doubt in her that wouldn't ever go away. That, from now on, she might just be waiting for him to lose his cool again and it would validate what he'd always thought about himself all along—that he wasn't a white-hat kind of guy in the least.

He was just about to put on his work gloves when she slid open the door and walked onto the concrete patio. She had already changed into a comfortable pair of pink sweats and Ugg boots, her hair in a ponytail.

"I forgot to thank you for the Valentine greetings," she said, gesturing toward the lights. The red box he'd picked up at a drugstore was gone, and he guessed that she'd put it inside.

"It was nothing," he said.

"Wrong. It was wonderful." She idly kicked at a piece of mulch that had strayed from the garden, tucking her hands into the front pockets of her sweatshirt. "You've been working like a dog lately. Why don't you take a night off and come inside for a sec?"

"I took a long break last night."

"You were decorating my backyard. I'd call that work." She stepped back over her threshold. "I bought some pink cupcakes with red sprinkles on top. Live a little, won't you?"

Cupcakes. It'd been a long time since he'd had any of those. Besides, she was making a peace offering to him, showing him that there were no hard feelings left over from this afternoon.

He'd take it.

Once they were inside, she showed him to her sofa. The red box with its white ribbon was indeed in a place of honor, right next to the TV, which was playing some Charlie Brown special with hearts and Snoopy all over the place.

As she brought over the cupcakes and some coffee, he noticed a few things. There was some kind of special cocoa-and-shea-butter lotion on the leather chest that she used as a coffee table. There was a pile of books about being a parent, too, alongside Tony Amati's journal.

The last thing he saw as she sat down was that, in the mug she'd kept for herself, there wasn't any coffee.

She noticed that he'd noticed. "Herbal tea," she said.

"Is that what all your books tell you to drink?" He motioned with his mug toward her minilibrary.

"They suggest it, and I'm nothing if not a good student."

"You think they studied up on childbirth back in the Stone Age?"

"Oh, don't even say that. I can't imagine what those poor women had to go through." She leaned back, her tummy like a cute, rounded ball peeking out from under her sweatshirt. "I'm starting to get nervous enough as it is, even with all the modern conveniences."

"You don't come off as being anxious."

"I try not to show it. What's the use?"

"I suppose there's not much of one." He wrinkled his brow. "So what're you going to do about having the baby? I mean, is there anyone to take you to the hospital and all that stuff?"

She raised her eyebrows, looking somewhat shy. "I was just starting to plan for that."

Was she going to ask *him?*

His nerves jittered. Maybe, if he told her straight out that he was the last person who should be acting like a caretaker, she would make some real plans, asking one of her coworkers or neighbors to help out.

But...

He glanced at that tummy, so round and touchable. He had put his palm over his ex-wife's stomach a time or two when she'd been pregnant, but he'd been absent most of the time on the rodeo circuit.

It was as if the heat of his glance made Annette itch, because she absently scratched her belly. "We never did talk about why you were putting that ex-miner in his place this afternoon."

"Is that why you invited me inside for cupcakes?"

She smiled. "I appreciate what you were doing. I've never really had anyone stand up for my honor before."

Again, with the white hat thing. Guilt pressed down on him.

"I'm not sure who started the rumor," she said, her cheeks going pink, "but you know what? I actually don't mind. I mean, at least not as far as *I* go. I can handle a little airy chatter, because it's far better than what I would've had to deal with when it came to Brett. But I feel bad that you've been pulled into it."

"Don't worry about me." He watched as she scratched at her tummy again. "I couldn't care less about an unvarnished reputation."

He wrinkled his brow. What exactly did he mean by that? Didn't he care that some folks in St. Valentine thought he might be the father?

As the thought settled, he was even more puzzled. Truthfully, he didn't care. It would mean that a woman like Annette had accepted him into her life, and how could that ever be a bad thing for him?

Shaking himself out of it, he pointed to her tummy as she kept scratching.

"You okay?" he asked.

"Oh." She stilled her hands, allowing them to rest on the sides of her belly. "My skin's expanding, and the itchiness is starting to drive me nuts."

He leaned forward, put down his coffee and grabbed the lotion. "I assume that's what this is for."

"Thanks." She took it from him.

When she opened the lid and squeezed, a bunch of lotion blooped out, and she startled as he put his hand under hers, catching the excess lotion as it dripped from her hand.

He took the bottle from her. "There's enough here to paint the side of a barn."

"I appreciate that observation."

His laugh was easy. "I'm not comparing you to one."

"Well, I'm starting to feel as big, and my bump's just going to get huger."

He helped her put the lotion back into the bottle, and she started to get up from the sofa.

"Where're you off to?" he asked.

"I…"

"For heaven's sake, Annie, your stomach's been peeping out of your sweatshirt all night. I've seen a little skin."

She cozied back into the cushions. "I didn't want to assume."

Assume what? That he was as curious about her tummy as he'd been about kissing her the first time and that another line would be crossed?

It was as if she'd suddenly gone shy as she leaned back and rubbed some lotion over her belly, making circles.

Making him far more curious than he'd hoped he would be.

As he watched out of the corner of his eye, he imagined his own hands on her, rubbing, feeling her flesh under his palms as he lulled her and comforted her.

A pain from the past shot through him—a piercing that ricocheted and echoed, showing him just how empty he was. He'd missed so much by being an absentee dad.

Yet now…

Annette must've seen the look on his face because she wrinkled her brow.

Was she wondering if he was thinking about his adoption? About how he'd acted in the nursery that day because he was supposedly smarting about how his parents had given him away?

Even if she misinterpreted the details, she had the rest of him nailed when she took him by the hand and laid his palm on her belly.

He didn't move.

"It's okay," she said quietly. But there was something else in her tone, too.

Something like longing.

The feel of bare skin and the firm roundness of a child beneath his hand tugged at him. His throat got clogged, and he couldn't say a word.

"Jared, it's really okay," she repeated on a whisper.

Not thinking of anything but the warmth that was stealing through him, he moved his hand back and forth, the lotion making her skin so smooth. She sighed as he gently touched her baby, touched her.

And he kept rubbing the lotion in, getting used to the intimacy, even the innocence of this moment.

"Have you thought of a name yet?" he finally asked.

But when he glanced at her again, her eyes were closed, her breath deep and even.

She'd fallen asleep.

He brought his hand away, suddenly realizing what he'd been doing—getting too close.

Way too close.

Carefully, he pulled her legs up onto the sofa so that she lay lengthwise on it, then fetched the chenille blanket from the back and tucked it around her.

Then he took one last look at her before he forced himself to retreat outside, to a near distance, where he truly belonged.

Chapter Seven

On the night of her mother's birthday, Annette left the Orbit Diner at four o'clock—enough time for her to go home and bake the same cake she did every year in remembrance of the mother who'd raised her pretty much by herself.

As she drove to her condo, she tried not to think about how she'd told her coworkers that she had plans with some so-called out-of-town family. It was a fib, of course, but she hadn't wanted anyone to feel sorry for her.

And she hadn't wanted anyone to pry.

Instead, she tried to get excited about the whole-grain macaroni and cheese with broccoli and ham dinner she was going to put together to enjoy in front of the TV, watching a bunch of DVDs she'd rented. Funny movies, romantic ones—a whole marathon that would make her remember how her mom used to laugh, or even when she had friends who used to come over and celebrate this day with her back in Tulsa. Contacting those friends in person was just too risky, even if she had sent them emails telling them that she was okay.

Most of all, though, tonight's movie marathon would help her not think about Jared.

She hadn't seen him for a few days—not since she'd let him touch her belly. He'd just seemed so... Was *freaked out* the phrase she was looking for? Because, when she'd woken up from her nap, he'd been outside, doing his digging and staying out there late into the moonlit night, well beyond the time she'd finally gone to bed. He'd managed to avoid her at the diner, too, although she'd seen more evidence of his digging outside her backyard fence as proof that he was still coming by the condo.

She turned her car onto Horizon Road, the last of the day's winter sun brushing the fields and fences that rolled by.

If she'd scared Jared off, she thought, then it was probably meant to be. And, really, shouldn't that point have been driven home to her the other day when she'd seen him with that ex-miner in town, shoving the man up against a wall?

Yes, it was true that all Jared had been doing was defending her. She even appreciated that fact. But the very sight of him angry, threatening...

Lord, the last thing she wanted to believe was that Jared was anything like Brett. That every man she met from here on out had it in him to lift a hand and strike out at someone, just as her ex-fiancé had almost done with her.

But when she'd told Jared her fears, there'd been sorrow in his gaze. A look that she would almost call brokenhearted.

Not knowing what to make of him, Annette turned into the driveway of her condo complex, motoring past the guest parking places and—

She sucked in a breath.

A familiar green truck had just backed out of a space and was coming toward her.

Jared was behind the wheel, and when he saw her, he put on his brakes.

She slowed, her heart racing a mile a minute. Was he going to take off without saying anything? It sure looked like it as he just sat there.

But, as she pulled up to him, he rolled down his window, leaning his arm on it, his face just as unreadable as ever.

She rolled down her window, too. "Done for the night, I suppose."

"I had the day off at the ranch, so I thought my time would be best spent out here."

While she was at the diner, huh? "Did you make any progress?"

"Not so much."

The sound of their engines filled the pause.

She found herself talking, even though she hadn't meant to. "It's my mom's birthday."

"Your mom?" He hesitated, then said, "I thought she…"

"She did. But I still celebrate even though she's gone. Maybe because she was one of the best things that ever happened to me."

And, still, they just idled there.

Good heavens, what was with him?

He stared out of his windshield as he planted one hand on the steering wheel. "I should probably let you go then."

Her heart sank, but why? What did she expect out of him?

She patted her stomach and smiled, letting him off the hook. "It'll be nice to spend tonight with my best buddy."

Why did he look somewhat pained by her answer?

He still didn't say goodbye yet, so she asked, "What're you up to?"

"I'm going to Gran's house. She whipped up a big meal, even though it's just for the two of us. She says I can take the leftovers to my bachelor pad and eat them for the next week."

"It sounds like she takes good care of you." Annette smiled.

"Yeah. Family is supposed to take care of each other, aren't they?" He gripped his steering wheel with that one hand while tilting up his hat with the other.

"Well," she said, "you have a fun time with Gran."

"Wait." He looked straight ahead again, as if making some huge decision.

Annette finally understood why he hadn't zoomed off yet. He felt bad that she and the baby would be alone tonight on this sad day, didn't he?

But wouldn't she feel the same about him if he was marking a sad night and didn't have a grandma around?

"Listen," he said. "Gran has all that food. Why don't you come over?"

"It's okay, Jared."

She wanted him to mean it when he invited her somewhere.

"Come on, Annie. You and Gran would get along, and she'd be tickled to have the company." He laughed softly. "She's an independent cuss, but I think she secretly loves to be around people. She sure brightens up whenever I come by."

Annette had to admit that she was curious about what any grandma of Jared's might be like. And the stories his gran might be able to tell about him.

Wouldn't that be worth a trip?

Besides, the more she thought about her mom's birthday, the sadder she got. She wasn't sure how long her mom would want her to be like that, baking that cake, remembering her, staying alone and shutting everyone else out.

"Just say yes," he said.

This time, it sounded as if he meant it, and that made all the difference.

"What time is she expecting you?" Annette asked.

Jared grinned and, for a moment, she wondered if he'd actually been hoping she would say yes the entire time.

After Jared had come with her into the condo and had gone to wash up in Annette's second bathroom, she went to her room and doffed her waitress uniform. She freshened up, then put on a "gently used" thrift-store long red velvet skirt with a frilly white top, both of which gave her stomach ample space. She put on some cheap but cute fake pearls and pinned up her hair, then came out to find Jared slumped on the sofa, thumbing through Tony's journal.

When he saw her, he slowly rose to his feet, taking off his hat.

He was looking at her as if she were wearing real pearls instead of someone's secondhand costume jewelry, and she could feel herself blushing from head to toe.

Putting down the journal, he seemed to recover. "You shine up nicely, Annie."

"Thank you."

Thud...thud... Her pulse was telling her everything that her mind had taken such a long time to accept—that she liked being looked at by Jared. A lot.

She went to the kitchen, grabbing a bottle of nonalcoholic sparkling berry cider she'd bought a few days ago and stuffing it into a tote bag. "You sure your grandma won't mind that I'm tagging along?"

"I called her already, and she's over the moon to have the company. There'll even be some friends from her church dropping by. She's got some sort of knitting group, and as much as it pains me, she does like to show me off to them."

Annette didn't say that Gran was probably eager to see what kind of woman Jared was hanging around with, besides.

"One thing before we go," she said, opening a kitchen drawer and pulling out a little red-striped box. She walked over to him, handing it over.

"What's this?"

"A gift."

"For what?"

She folded her arms over her chest. "Valentine lights? Box of chocolates? I felt like returning the favor."

"This wasn't necessary."

It occurred to her that he hadn't been expecting anything in return for his kindness.

"Go ahead then," she said, laughing. "Boy, you have a hard time with gifts, don't you?"

Finally he tore into the present. She took the paper from him and crumbled it in her hand, waiting, anticipating his reaction.

After opening the box, he slowly pulled out an old-fashioned tarnished silver watch hanging from a chain.

"I saw it at a vintage store a while ago," she said. "I wasn't thinking it would be a thank-you gift, but it looks like the kind of watch Tony would wear, and I couldn't resist."

He seemed gobsmacked that he had randomly crossed her mind like that, thinking of him when she didn't have to.

"Thank you, Annie," he said simply, but the pleasure and softness of his tone said so much more.

She could tell that he was wondering if he should hug her or not, so she took matters in hand and embraced him before the moment passed.

"It'll look great on you," she said as she held him to her.

His arms slid up her back, and they stood like that for a few seconds. She even closed her eyes, wishing she could just stay here in his arms all night.

But he let her go, clearing his throat. He held up the watch, as if the hug had never happened.

"I think it goes a little something like this," he said, clipping one end of the chain to his waistband and putting the watch in his front pocket.

He did wear it well, and she stifled her wild heartbeat as he led her to the door.

She almost—but not quite—forgot that she wouldn't be baking her mom's cake tonight as they drove about ten minutes out of town, their journey ending on a country lane where sweeps of lawn separated the houses from the road. Jared pulled into the driveway of what Annette imagined might be the home of the baker's wife in a fairy tale, with window boxes blooming with perennial flowers and lacy trim around the eaves. Because it was out of St. Valentine, it wasn't decorated for the festival, but it was festive enough as it was.

Once they'd gone to the door and knocked, Annette smiled at Jared. "Everything's so cute."

He didn't have time to respond before the door was opened by a small, wiry, tomboyish woman with a long silver braid and wearing a denim skirt and a flower-embroidered cardigan.

"Here they are!" she said, hugging Jared.

Even with his grandma he clearly wasn't all that used to hugs, but he held her an instant longer than an average grandma embrace required.

He was getting used to showing affection, Annette thought, holding back another smile.

"Gran," he said, pulling back, "this is my friend Annette."

She didn't react to how she was "Annette" now instead of "Annie." The lack of a nickname sounded so darn formal.

She took Gran's outstretched hand and shook it, but the other woman lay her palm on top of Annette's hand, squeezing.

"It's a pleasure to meet you and have you at my house tonight, Annette."

"Thank you so much for having me."

As she brought them into the house, the aroma of cinnamon, cloves and ham stirred Annette's senses. It smelled like home, where someone was always there to welcome you with a meal they'd carefully made, hoping you would like it.

The kind of meal her mom would have cooked, once upon a time.

After Jared and Annette took off their coats and his hat and hung them on a rack by the door, Annette handed over the sparkling cider to Gran. Then their hostess ushered them into her family room. Hors d'oeuvres were already on the coffee table, including a cheese ball with crackers, sliced vegetables, crockpot meatballs and a layered dip with tortilla chips.

Gran said, "It's too bad you've got a bun baking in that oven, Annette. I've got some hooch you would've loved."

Annette wasn't so used to people coming right out with the pregnancy observations. But it was refreshing. "I wish I could have some, but the sparkling cider's good for tonight."

"Coming right up."

Jared and Annette sat on a couch with doilies on the back. He watched his grandma leave, then grabbed a little paper plate decorated with more flowers.

"What's your pleasure?" he asked.

Annette had to remind herself that he was talking about the food, not anything else.

He was only being nice in bringing you here, she reminded herself. *Don't think it's anything more.*

"How about a bit of everything?" Annette said. "Not too much, though. I shouldn't load up before dinner."

Jared began to fill her plate as Doris Day played on

low volume from the stereo system, which looked like it had been around since the 1970s.

"Your gran's a spitfire, isn't she?" she asked.

"Slightly. I think retirement is driving her nuts. She used to run a cattle ranch with my granddad back in the day."

"Did you ever know your grandpa?"

"Nope. I just found Gran several months ago, but he had passed on a while back. That seems to drive her bonkers, too—not having anyone around."

Gran's voice came from the back of the house, where the kitchen probably was. "I admit to liking some company!"

Jared kept filling up Annette's plate. "Did I mention her eerily fantastic hearing?"

She bustled into the room, somehow balancing two puppy-decorated mugs and a champagne glass teeming with sparkling cider all at one time. She delivered Annette's drink first.

"My hearing's always been sharp," she said.

"Some would say that your conversation can be rather pointed, too," Jared said, glancing at Annette's tummy as he handed over her hors d'oeuvres, then began working on a plate of his own.

"What about it?" Gran said, sitting in a chair nearby. "Was I wrong to say something about the baby?"

"No," Annette said, after sipping from her glass. "People have just started to notice because I recently got bigger."

"Then why not say something?" Gran shrugged. "Straightforwardness only saves time."

And she forged ahead from there, asking Annette

baby details: When was the child expected, what was the sex, what names was she thinking of?

Before she could ask why Annette didn't have a ring on her finger, Jared interrupted, and she got the feeling that he'd warned Gran when he'd called her earlier about going too far.

"So," he said. "I'd say you kind of like entertaining, Gran."

She seemed to get the hint, and she winked at him. "Yes, I do. I have to say that I'm enjoying this dinner far more with you here, Jared. And you, Annette."

She might have just been being nice with that last part, but, in a way, Annette thought she might very well mean it. Gran seemed happy to have her grandson here with someone who was obviously comfortable around him.

Heck, Annette was probably the only person who was comfortable with him in the entire town of St. Valentine.

Gran put down her hooch on the coffee table and started to fill an hors d'oeuvre plate.

"I hope you don't think I'm a lonely old biddy," Gran said. "For years, I've volunteered at my church. On Sundays, we visit the houses of homebound parishioners all day, and it's a kick to see my old friends. But there was never anything or anyone otherwise. Not until now."

She sent a fond smile to them, and Annette's heart teemed with warmth.

Three people in this very room who might've been alone, except…they weren't.

She caught Jared gazing at her, and her pulse gave a start.

Was he thinking the same thing?

He looked away, and Annette's heart contracted a little. Why did he always have to pull back just when he was getting close?

Gran's voice was soft when she added, "Yes, I am very happy you found me, boy."

Nodding, he said, "I'm happy, too, Gran."

Annette ran a piece of celery through the dip on her plate, just for something to do, especially as Gran went on.

"Lord knows," she said, "that it took a lot of courage for Jared to hunt down my whereabouts, seeing as his mom—my own daughter—didn't give him all that much encouragement when he found *her*."

Annette stopped with the celery and risked a look at Jared. He'd told her that he was adopted, but he hadn't ever said anything about meeting his birth mom.

He had stiffened, putting down his mug and plate, not looking at Annette.

There was something even deeper and darker going on with him than she'd ever guessed, wasn't there?

Gran sank back in her chair. "There I go with the straightforwardness again."

"It's all right, Gran," he said.

Annette began to slide to the edge of the couch, preparing to leave them alone. "Maybe I should—"

"No," he said. "Don't. I could've said something to you before, but I didn't think it was a big deal."

Didn't he realize that everything about him had become a big deal to her?

She pressed her lips together as Gran spoke.

"My own daughter," she said, "doesn't deserve Jared. That sounds terrible coming from me, but when she got pregnant with him, she wasn't prepared. She was fourteen years old and hell on wheels. Hardly equipped to have a child then, and I doubt it's changed much now."

Annette could feel Jared's gaze on her, as if gauging her thoughts. It shocked her that he wanted her to know all this, especially after all his tenderfooting around.

Had she been wrong about him not being very interested in her after all?

So she said to Gran, "It sounds like you haven't seen your daughter in a while."

"Not since she left home all those years ago, but it wasn't for my lack of trying to see her. She just always needed to do her own thing, and…" Gran's voice cracked. "She went and did it, deserting whoever Jared's father was, too. She never did have a permanent address or home, just floated through life."

Gran picked up her cup again, staring into it before drinking.

When Jared spoke, his tone was gentle, as if he were far more worried about how his birth mom's attitude had affected his grandma than himself. "She doesn't know what she missed by leaving you, Gran."

She finished drinking. "She was a fool to have treated you the way she did, too. I told you before that I would've taken you in had she stayed around long enough for me to know she was having a baby. And, even though we learn how to forgive in church, I have a hard time doing it. You're my only grandchild, and she took you away from me. Then she turned you away that second time, after you found her."

Annette fully turned to Jared, and the sight of him twisted something inside of her. His jaw was tight, as if he were warding off every bit of emotion that was trying to take him over.

No wonder he was how he was.

Without thinking, she put a hand on her belly. Jared saw the movement, and his gaze landed there.

His eyes traveled up to hers, and there was such devastation in him that she wanted to reach out, bring him into her embrace and never let go.

She'd been so wrong when she'd seen him confront that ex-miner. This man didn't hurt people.

This man just hurt.

Annette wasn't sure what to say now, and she was certain that everyone in the room was feeling the same way until there was a murmur of voices outside on the porch, then a knock on the door.

Gran sprang out of her chair, as if grateful for the interruption. When she opened the door, a crowd of women carrying big bags full of yarn surged inside to hug her.

While Gran introduced them as friends from her church, Annette smiled, welcoming a bit of cheer.

And, when she rested her palm on top of Jared's hand on the couch, she felt even cheerier as he turned his hand over, clasping hers.

The ride back to Annette's house seemed to take forever for Jared.

He could sense all the questions she had for him about his birth mom because, after Gran's friends had shown up, the mood had shifted and the uncomfortable discussion had gone by the wayside. To boot, a couple of her church pals had unexpectedly stayed for dinner after she'd impetuously invited them, and that had given Jared a further reprieve.

It was his fault that the whole discussion had started

anyway because he hadn't stopped Gran from introducing it. Deep down, had he wanted Annette to know?

And, now that she did, was he in way too deep with her, in spite of all his efforts to stay distant?

He parked the pickup in a guest space. Gran had sent home an army of Tupperware containers brimming with food, and Annette couldn't possibly carry all of it in on her own.

As they came to her front door, arms loaded, she said, "You should really keep all of this, Jared."

"I never told Gran that I'm not one to eat leftovers. Besides, I've got my schedule down—lunch at the diner whenever I'm in town and dinner at the Queen of Hearts."

He'd grabbed her keys before she'd gotten out of the truck, and now he unlocked the door, then pushed it open, waiting for her to go in first.

As she passed, he smelled the flowery shampoo she used, and even a trace of the cocoa-and-shea butter. It brought back with a slam the feel of her bare stomach beneath his hand.

The aftermath of the memory tingled in his belly as he followed her to the kitchen and set down the containers.

"At the very least," she said, "you've got to help me eat all this when you're over here digging. Even if I'm working, I'll just give you a key so you can come in when you need to."

He was about to refuse her, but then she turned those beautiful blue eyes on him, and he was dust.

"Sounds good," he said.

"Great." She opened the fridge, putting the food inside.

He could almost feel the moment her thoughts turned, getting serious as she closed the door then slid off her coat and draped it on the counter.

"About earlier…"

"You don't have to say a word about it."

"But I want to." She motioned with her hands, almost helplessly. "You can't care about someone and not care about what happened to them in the past. This thing with your mom—"

"My *birth* mom." He'd corrected her before checking himself.

"Right." A heartbeat of time passed. "I just… What did your grandma mean when she said that your birth mom turned you away a second time?"

He realized this conversation would require some time, so he took off his hat, shrugged off his coat and put them on the counter, too.

Then, he started.

"I found out I was adopted when I stumbled on a letter from the man I'd been calling 'Dad' all the years I was growing up," he said. "My parents had passed on by then, and I was living with a bachelor uncle who'd taken me in. Long story short, after I left that home, I eventually got curious enough to hire a private investigator, and he found my birth mom living with some guy in Birmingham. It was probably a temporary arrangement because that seems to be her M.O."

"And then you went to meet her?"

"It was the stupidest thing I've ever done." But that wasn't true. There was an even stupider decision in his life that he couldn't bear the thought of revealing to Annette—the abandonment of his own daughter.

Annette took a step toward him, and he didn't go anywhere.

"Every child wants to know about their parents," she said. "With my dad dying when I was young, all I wanted was to somehow meet him again, even though I knew it wasn't possible. If I'd had the chance, I would've jumped at it."

"Well, when I found her, she wasn't exactly overwhelmed with joy, like your dad would've been."

"What did she do?"

God, he'd never told every single detail to anyone, not even Gran.

"At first, after I told her who I was, she just stood there in her doorway," he said, the words scratching out of his throat. "In that space of time, I remember thinking that I didn't resemble her that much. That I must've inherited my eyes and hair from my dad. Then she got this look on her face, and she said, 'You shouldn't have come here.'"

Annette seemed stricken. "All those years apart, and that's what she told you?"

"She had a few more good ones. When I asked about my dad, she told me she didn't even know who he was. There were a few candidates, she said, and she gave me up for adoption so she wouldn't have to be reminded of any of us again."

"She said that?"

Jared nodded, unsure that he could utter another word. As Annette lay a tender hand on his arm, he broke down.

"She never even invited me inside," he whispered, so roughly that it came out sounding as though he was being ripped apart.

But it was as if that rip had opened up something new, and he thought it might be relief.

And when he saw that Annette wasn't judging him, that she was only looking at him with an affection he'd never thought to find in any person, he knew it went even beyond relief.

"All these years," she said, resting her fingertips against his cheek, "you've been carrying this around inside of you. Most people wouldn't be able to stand that, Jared."

He wanted to answer that most people might not have had any sparkle of hope to keep them going—the thought that, maybe, there *were* good people in his past. That his birth mom was the only hideous stain on this new existence he'd found.

That maybe, a possible blood relation like Tony Amati might show him where he was headed by revealing where he'd been.

It was as if, right now, Annette was the only person who'd ever understand all of that.

She whispered, "Just know that the day you came into my life, you changed it for the better. You're the best man I know."

He wasn't so sure about that, but the doubt dissipated as she stroked his cheek.

And the world went fuzzy as he gathered her in his arms and kissed her, needing her more than he'd ever needed anything or anyone.

Chapter Eight

She was his.

As Jared wrapped his arms around her, encompassing her as if she belonged only to him and he wasn't ever going to let her go, she gave herself fully over, knowing that it was always meant to be this way.

Back when he'd first walked into the diner all those months ago, through the summer and fall and beginning of winter, as they'd bantered and kept a friendly yet polite space between them, this moment had been coming.

It had been inevitable.

And she reveled in every bit of it, kissing him right back, sinking against his wide chest, hooking her arms under his and gripping his shoulders, feeling her baby bump nestling against him.

During their first kiss, there'd been a sense of innocence, but not now—not after such an emotionally charged night when he'd been laid bare to her.

Now there was raw urgency as his mouth devoured hers, as he claimed her and she opened herself to him.

She moaned as he slowed the kiss, as his tongue entered her mouth, seeking, needing, stroking her tongue with a knee-weakening rhythm.

She felt hotter with every roiling bang of her pulse as it pounded in her chest, sliding down and down until it got to the middle of her legs.

She ached for him—ached until she had to break off their kiss and bury her face in his neck.

Skin and musk and cowboy, she thought again, her breath heavy and ragged against him. Her mouth pressed against a vein, and she could feel it throbbing beneath her lips, could feel his heart beating crazily in his chest.

He buried his fingers in her hair, loosening the pins that were holding it up. "Annie?"

It was a question, maybe not just to her.

Even just by saying her name, she could hear all his confusion. Should he go any further?

Should *they?*

She'd already come up with an answer on the night she'd returned home to find her backyard decorated with lights that were just as bright as what she felt in her heart right now. That night, she had seen in Jared a man who could love, and he had been nothing like the guy she had feared he might be—too full of secrets, too removed to ever have significant feelings for anyone else.

So should they?

"Yes," she whispered.

His breath hitched as he held her away from him, searching her gaze. She smiled up at him while he pulled the pins from her hair, one by one. They dropped to the floor with what sounded like tiny chimes.

When he was done, her hair fell down her back and her shoulders, and he pushed it away from her face, exploring her temples, her cheekbones, her jawline.

It was as if he'd never seen her before, and maybe he hadn't—not like this, at least. Not so vulnerable, with her refusing to hide how she felt about him now.

Two people who could've been alone tonight, she thought, leaning against one of his palms as he cupped her face. *Two people who belong together.*

Even though she'd said yes to him, he still seemed hesitant to go on.

So she helped him along.

She reached up, undoing the first button on his shirt. The second. Then pulling the material out of his jeans so she could undo the rest.

He sucked in a breath as she spread open his shirt.

There was a sprinkling of hair over his chest, which was just as muscled and firm as she'd imagined it would be. She pressed her hands to him, and it felt so good— better than it could have with any other man.

Just look at him, she thought. He was worth a million men, and she wanted to show him that.

She slipped off his shirt, and it seemed as if he was letting her take the lead.

That felt good, too, because she'd never really been the type to do that before. Maybe it was because she'd never wanted something—or someone—this badly.

She'd heard that women who were as pregnant as she was might be too tired for sex or might feel too unattractive, but damn were they wrong.

His arms were bunched with muscles, and just out of

pure desire, she walked around him, trailing her hand over his chest, his arm, until she came to his back.

And...damn.

She'd never imagined anyone could look like this, his shoulders wide, his deltoids rippling as he reached for the counter, as if her mere touch were enough to send him falling.

She had studied art, lived through art during school, but she'd lost all sense of that lately...until now.

He was a masterpiece.

Tracing her fingers over the lines of him, she explored his back, his sides, then lower, coaxing her fingers into the waistband of his dark jeans.

"Annie..." he said again, a jagged warning.

As if he was going to stop her now. "For a man of few words, there's sure a lot of chatter coming from you."

She leaned her face against his back—all warm, smooth skin, muscle, male—and slipped her fingers farther into the side of his jeans.

He made a pleased yet tortured sound, but she barely heard it as she felt his hip—hard yet soft, sculpted by all the manual labor he did every day.

"You're all a woman could ever want," she said, drawing her hand to his front, where his abs clenched under her butterfly touch.

She skimmed her fingertips upward, over the fine line of hair that disappeared into his belly button, then went back down, pausing over the snap of his jeans.

The point of no return.

Her life flashed before her eyes: the bad decisions she had made, the bridal gown that had been stuffed in the trunk of her car, the blank walls of this condo when she had first entered it with nothing more than a positive attitude to her name.

Then this—a good decision. The best she would ever make.

She unbuttoned his fly with deliberate care, feeling his belly jump, feeling his breathing quicken. Her own breath was warm and damp against his back while she rested her forehead against him.

Then, as he made a guttural sound, she eased her hand over his hardness, her heartbeat taking her over with a palpitating fever.

He cursed as he put his hand over hers, holding her to him. But then he turned around and, with one fluid move, clutched the bottom of her frilly white blouse and started unbuttoning it from there on up.

Her first instinct was to stop him. She'd gained so much weight. It'd been one thing to see him without a stich of clothing, but it was another to have her bared to his gaze.

But he didn't seem to care as he peeled open her blouse to expose her major-league bullet bra.

Her breasts spilled over the cups, and a hungry heat took over his gaze.

"Annie, you're so beautiful."

Moved by that, she let him take off her blouse, then unhook the back of her bra.

It fell to the kitchen floor, and she almost covered herself with her arms before he tenderly put his hands on her shoulders.

"Don't," he said quietly. Then stronger. "Don't."

Her head spun as he mapped her as thoroughly as she'd done to him, his hands lightly smoothing over her arms, then cupping her breasts. He rubbed his thumbs over her nipples, bringing them to beaded peaks.

Then he did something she'd never thought any man would do to her—he took her in his arms and romantically dipped her back just enough so that he latched his mouth to a nipple, sucking.

She threaded her fingers through his dark hair, holding back a cry. Every pull of his mouth hurt, but in such a good way that she could hardly stand it. Her body agreed with her, too, as a twist spiraled between her legs, traveling higher, higher, until she was tugging at his hair with every one of his pulls and nips.

He loved her with his mouth, sending her up, pushing her higher and higher.

She made a helpless sound as a tiny explosion threatened, sharp and straining but not quite there yet.

When he looked at her face, he no doubt saw how flushed she was, how on the edge she was of something even bigger. In one fluid motion he scooped her into his arms and carried her out of the kitchen, down the hall, toward her bedroom.

Out of oxygen, she could barely talk. "My bed... It's..."

They came through the door, and he set her down on her feet, where she swayed against him, both of them staring at her twin bed.

But he wasted no time in stripping off the covers, the sheets, grabbing pillows and tossing them to the floor on top of it all.

"What're you doing?" she asked.

He slipped his thumb into the expandable waistband of her velvet skirt, working it downward. "I'm not taking a chance on that bed."

It was too small—made only for a single girl—but that didn't seem to matter when they had a makeshift place on the floor that was just as good.

When he had her skirt and boots off, he lay her down, propping pillows behind her.

Then, as she panted, almost dying because she wanted him so badly, he stripped.

When he reached into his jeans pocket, she thought he might be searching for a condom.

"No need for that," she said. "Unless…"

He assured her that there was no other reason for protection, and when he came to her, she was ready for him.

She was propped up by the pillows, and he made sure that his weight wasn't on her belly as he braced himself over her.

"My Annie," he said.

She was about to answer, but he entered her before she could speak, and her words were sucked in on a breath.

He filled her, and as he moved in, out, gently, slowly at first, she held on to him, looking into his dark gaze.

There was an unfathomable fire there, so deep that she felt as if she was going into a place that swallowed her whole and burned her at the edges, singeing, searing as she took him all the way in.

The climax she'd been so close to earlier flickered in her, building, licking until she had to close her eyes and grab harder on to him.

The faster he went, the more he fanned the fire hotter, higher, till the flames were so fierce and blazing, they lit up that dark place until she saw everything about him, about them, about—

As the orgasm consumed her, her last thought floated by, spinning away from her until she could barely grasp it.

But she did catch it. And it was only then that she knew just what it was.

Love.

She had definitely fallen in love with the man in black.

After they'd made love, Jared watched Annette in the moonlight that arced through the window. She'd fallen asleep, cuddled against him, but he couldn't catch a wink.

Wasn't it the guy who was supposed to slumber off after sex?

But Annette had seemed satisfied—no, ecstatic—with what had gone on between them, so her exhaustion didn't bother him. Nothing much did at the moment, as a matter of fact, because he was the happiest he'd ever been.

When they'd started to make love, he'd had an instant of doubt, but it had soon been erased when she'd urged him to a point where he couldn't stop himself from being with her. She was everything he'd ever wanted in a woman, and he still couldn't believe that she'd given herself to him.

She sighed in her sleep, and he brushed a piece of moonbeam hair away from her face. Every breath she took was like his own, and he couldn't get enough of her.

Yet, soon enough, he began to feel a heaviness on his shoulders again.

A reminder that he hadn't told her everything.

Just because she knew about him being rejected by

his birth mom didn't mean she would understand what he'd done in the past. She still didn't know the ugliest reality about him.

She rolled to her side, toward him, slipping an arm over his hip. His flesh tingled where she touched it, and that overwhelming affection for her he'd felt earlier seized him again. Without thinking, he lay back, putting his arms around her as she breathed against him, her belly fitting against him perfectly.

He must've fallen asleep like that because, before he knew it, he was awake and morning was peeping in the curtains.

Annette was still cuddled against him, her eyes closed, a lazy smile on her face.

Had she been dreaming about him?

When she opened one eye and smiled even wider, he was pretty sure that she'd been awake for a while.

"Morning," she whispered.

"Morning to you, too."

He kept holding her, wondering if she was going to change her mind about being so close to him.

But when she planted a kiss on his nose, then snuggled against him, he accepted it for as long as the guilt would allow him to.

Just as he thought she might fall back asleep, she groaned and said, "Darn," then shrugged out of the blankets and got to her feet, naked as the morning.

He couldn't look away from her shapely, gorgeous body: long legs, curvy hips, round belly, swollen breasts. He guessed she'd had an hourglass figure before the pregnancy, but now she was even more breathtaking.

"One thing about having a baby," she said, "is the constant—"

She pointed toward the bathroom in the hall, and he understood.

As she left the room, she said, "I hope I didn't keep you up last night with all my getting up and down."

"Not at all." Maybe he'd slept like a log, after all, because he didn't remember any of that.

He heard a door close and wondered what he should do now. It was the morning after, and aside from his short marriage, he'd never stayed around for long with other women.

But Annette was anything but the usual.

He got up from the floor, put on his jeans, then decided that he should probably make the bed. It seemed a real polite thing to do and, for some reason, he thought it'd be a nice gesture.

Maybe he just wanted to hang around a little longer, though, and this was an excuse.

Whatever it was, Annette came back soon enough, tying the sash of a blue terry-cloth robe around her. She had whisked her hair up into a clip, exposing her neck.

Was it wrong that all Jared wanted to do was kiss it?

"You hungry for some breakfast?" she asked, chipper as could be. "Pancakes? Waffles?"

His stomach was getting a little rumbly, now that he thought about it. "Is all that stuff whole wheat and healthy?"

"I think there might be a decadent unhealthy waffle somewhere in the freezer. Terry left some food in there before he moved into his new house."

She glanced at the semimade bed and smiled at Jared, and he wasn't sure if it was because he'd been straightening the blankets back into place or because he'd helped her to muss it up last night.

At any rate, he followed her into the kitchen, where she rummaged in the freezer for those waffles, coming out with an ice-encrusted box.

"Didn't you luck out?" she asked, going to the toaster.

He found his shirt on the floor where he'd left it last night and shrugged back into it.

Were they ever going to talk about what'd happened? Or did Annette just assume that it was the first step in something more?

Just tell her everything about yourself before you get in too deep, he thought. *Then you can decide.*

But he feared he was in too deep already.

Deeper than he ever thought he'd be, and he didn't want to shatter everything good about that.

"So," she said, opening the fridge and bringing out a pitcher of orange juice, then a container of cherry yogurt and some kind of health-food syrup that he wouldn't dare complain about. After putting them on the table, she glanced at him, and for the first time this morning, she looked a little shy.

His stomach kicked, and gut instinct told him to play it cool. "Is this where I ask you what you're doing today?"

She laughed a little at his weaving and dodging. "You could do that."

"Then what're you doing today, Annie?"

She took some glasses out of a low cupboard, then some utensils from a drawer and placed them on the table, too. "I didn't have any big plans. But I did think that maybe this was a good time to start some new family traditions." She rubbed her stomach.

His hands itched, wanting to cradle her bump, too. "What kind of traditions?"

"A scrapbook, for one. Technically, this will be baby's first Valentine's Day coming up, even though he or she is still cave-bound."

"I guess you could make a Valentine page for him or her. One page for each year."

"See?" she said. "You're naturally good at this."

Before he could ask exactly what "this" meant— playing a game of Valentine's-Day-for-Baby or thinking like a parent?—the waffles popped out of the toaster and she went to put them on a plate.

"I was also thinking," she said, "of keeping a journal, just so my son or daughter could read it one day. I wish my parents had done that."

She brought the plate to him, and he looked up at her.

"Did you come up with that idea because of Tony's journal?" he asked.

She nodded, going to the stove, taking a teapot and filling it with water from the sink. All the while, Jared had the feeling that Annette was mulling over a heavier subject. He just didn't know what.

"Go ahead with whatever you want to say," he told her.

She didn't waste a second. "I've just been wondering... You've never come right out and told me why you're so into Tony Amati. I mean, I could guess, but I'd kind of like to hear it from you." She turned on the burner and put the kettle on. "If you want to tell me, that is."

He sat down and doused his waffles with syrup. His first thought was about how much he could tell her without totally revealing everything about himself.

His second thought was that he shouldn't be hiding anything. Not anymore.

But he couldn't let her know just what a white-hat kind of guy he wasn't, especially if he stayed around.

Good God, he was actually thinking that it was possible. A drifter like him, finally setting down some roots. Yet how could he stay around for her if he kept lying about what sort of man she was with?

He decided to give her as much as he could for now. "My fascination with Tony is complicated," he said as she filled his glass with juice.

"Isn't everything?"

She sat near him, and his body came alive, just as it had last night.

"The easiest way I can explain it is this," he said. "When you look in a mirror, you see your reflection. That's how we know who we are, right?"

"Right." She was looking at him, following every word he said closely.

"Well, Tony looks just like me. He's kind of a mirror, so to speak."

"Someone you feel close to."

"Exactly." This was easier than he thought it would be. "After I found out I was adopted, I hired that P.I., and after he tracked down my birth mom, he also looked into seeing if I had any other living relatives. I don't really know what I was doing, searching my past even after my birth mom rejected me... Maybe I was just trying to find *someone* out there who might want me in their lives."

Annette's smile told him that he'd found that in spades, and it gave him the courage to go on.

"When he told me that I had a grandma near Houston, I set out here, thinking I'd just meet her, appease my curiosity, then go on my way."

"It didn't quite turn out that way, though."

"No, it didn't." He grinned. "Gran isn't anything like her daughter. She was warm and accepting right off the bat."

"I wonder if that's because she knew what it was like for you to be turned aside by your birth mom because her daughter did the same thing to her."

"You're right. But the thing is, I kept letting Gran know that I wasn't going to stay around forever. I didn't want her to be disappointed when I left."

Annette went quiet, and it just about slayed him.

He leaned forward, using his finger to tip up her chin. "That was at the beginning, before I got to know you."

She brightened at that, and he hated himself. What if he ended up *not* staying? What if she was ultimately so disgusted by everything he had to tell her that she didn't even want him around?

He continued, refusing to think about the worst.

"Anyway, that brings us to Tony," he said. "I went into St. Valentine one day, into the Queen of Hearts Saloon, and there he was, on the wall in those pictures. I told you before that I asked Gran about him, but she said she didn't know all that much."

"And you don't believe that."

"No. People just don't randomly look alike, especially when Gran said my birth family has roots in this area that go way back. So that's why I'm still here. Because I'm going to get to the bottom of who he is and how I'm related to him."

She tilted her head. "But that's not all, is it? Tony, your mirror, can show you what you're made of. He can make you proud of who you are, unlike your birth mom."

Out of everyone in creation, Annette had understood. At least this part of his story.

"For a while," he said, "when I was young, I knew exactly who I was because I thought I knew who my parents were. But then I found out differently, and I realized that I had no idea about anything anymore."

"What about Gran? Isn't she enough to make you feel good about your new family?"

"Not when I have another me who once existed."

She smiled, taking it all in before saying, "I get it, Jared. It makes perfect sense to me."

Then she stood and went to the stove, totally content with his explanation, as if he'd told her everything.

Even though he hadn't.

Chapter Nine

It had been too much for them to stay away from each other for the rest of the day, and they'd ended up in one another's arms again, stretching out the hours, getting to know each other's bodies tenderly. Slowly.

Wonderfully.

In the end, though, after they'd showered and rested, Annette was just happy to have Jared by her side on the sofa, where she could lean over and put her head on his shoulder and hold on to his arm. She loved the feel of him—the strong muscles, the sense that he was with her and didn't want to be anywhere else.

He hadn't said as much, but she knew it had to be true from the way she would catch him looking at her with that craving in his gaze.

Yet, every so often, she had to admit that there was something else there, too, even though he'd revealed a big part of himself last night and this morning.

She could only guess that it had to do with something he still wanted to say to her, though he wasn't saying it.

But she'd always known that Jared wasn't a man to rush into matters. She would just give him time to come out with whatever he had to tell her.

All the time he needed.

After they ate some of Gran's leftovers for dinner, Jared seemed a little cabin feverish, so she suggested getting some air. And she knew the perfect place to go.

They drove to the Helping Hands Ranch, where the lights could be enjoyed from the ground, or from far above St. Valentine, just as she'd seen them with Jared the other night.

"I heard that a lot of news outlets picked up the internet broadcast," Annette told him as they walked toward a massive field located away from the corrals and stables, where disadvantaged kids spent their time tending to the horses and turning around their lives with the help of counselors. "This place has already become a piece of St. Valentine history."

The air was chillier than usual, and Annette had put on a pair of red gloves to go along with her coat. Jared walked next to her as they approached one of the displays—the cupids in flight.

From the ground, everything looked like a celestial maze of red and white bulbs, and as she brushed against him, he reached over, taking her hand in his, as if they were entering something unknown together.

A trill of adoration shot through her. "It's a little bit like heaven, isn't it?"

"As close as you can get to it on Earth, I suppose."

He was right because heaven was Jared, here, with

her now, being unafraid to show everyone that they were together.

They were an actual couple, Annette thought almost giddily. Somehow, she'd brought him out of that dark Black Bart shell he'd used for so long.

As they made their way to the middle of the cupids display, the white bulbs reflected in Jared's eyes like stars whenever she looked up into his gaze. He smiled down at her, and she forgot all those moments today when she had wondered what he might still be holding back.

And when he would say he wanted to stay with her forever.

Around them, folks were strolling down the illuminated lanes—people from town, whose gazes tracked Annette and Jared with curiosity, and tourists, who greeted them anonymously without minding who they were or what kind of gossip they would probably cause around St. Valentine now.

But Annette just smiled at every one of them, hardly caring about anything because life was that good.

They were just rounding a corner, coming upon the display of the cowgirl roping the cowboy, when they ran into the last people Jared probably cared to meet.

Davis and Violet Jackson had obviously taken the night off from the newspaper, enjoying some time together, and when they saw Jared and Annette, they slowed their steps.

"Evenin'," Davis said as they approached. His dark blond hair caught the lights, and his tailored suit and coat and fancy hand-tooled boots boasted that he had money to spare.

Although Violet was a hometown girl, she looked

just as cosmopolitan as her husband tonight, her red hair cut in a trendy style that skimmed her neck.

She sent Annette a grin because they'd always gotten along, then turned to Jared. "We didn't come here tonight to chase you through the lights, if that's what you're worried about. There's an unofficial interview moratorium in this maze."

Jared's voice was low. "I wish that sort of offer lasted outside it, too."

Annette didn't know how the reporters would react to Jared's gruffness, so when they chuckled, she was pretty surprised.

"Jared," Davis said, "if there were an easier way to uncover information about Tony Amati than asking you for it, Vi and I would be all over that."

"As it is," she said, "we've exhausted just about all of our options, although we've got one more lead to comb through."

So they were just about at the end of their ropes with Tony Amati, too, huh? Annette thought of all the upset dirt in the back of her condo.

Davis and Violet Jackson weren't the only ones coming up empty.

Jared had tightened his hold on her hand. "Maybe that's how Tony would have wanted things—private and dead-ended."

Davis said, "He would've wanted what was best for St. Valentine. If he could see what his mystery has done for the town's economy, I think he'd be happy."

"He might," Jared said, taking them all aback with the concession.

His hat had been riding low over his eyes, but he

pushed it up an inch. Davis and Violet both stood still, as if they'd never seen this much of Jared before.

As if he'd never shown anyone outside of Annette more than he'd needed to.

He kept holding her hand, and the reporters' gazes took that in, too. Were they seeing an entirely new man tonight?

Annette's heart warmed. He *was* different now, wasn't he? Because of her?

Jared continued, "Don't you have enough on Tony?"

"We're not much further than when we started," Violet said. "Even with all the work we've done, it's still as if Tony barely existed before he came to St. Valentine."

"But, as you said, it seems that's sufficient enough to bring in more business than the town's seen in years," Jared said. "People love what they don't know. That's why they've been lured here. It could be that giving them all the answers about Tony would crush the mystery and the draw."

Davis laughed. "You're talking to reporters, Jared. We live for answers."

Annette remembered those odd references in Tony's journal about having to start over here, and she was sure Jared was only doing his best to defend his probable ancestor in his own way.

But this also seemed to go into very personal territory for Jared. Was he asking Davis and Violet to back off more investigating because, subconsciously, *he* didn't want to know everything about Tony? Was he hoping that Tony had only done good deeds and that would finally bring him some pride?

Jared had told her that the man was like a mirror for him, a reflection that might help him find himself.

How awful would it be for him to discover that Tony hadn't been exaggerating about the "terrible sins" he'd mentioned in his journal?

It'd be one more slap in the face for a man who'd been beaten down his entire life, and Annette felt as defensive of Jared as he'd been of her with those dirty-mouthed ex-miners the other day.

She spoke up, and everyone locked gazes on her because she'd been quiet this entire time.

"All he's asking," she said, "is that you look at what you're doing with Tony and think about whether the answers would be worth shining an even bigger spotlight on a man who took a lot of pains to ensure his privacy."

Neither of the Jacksons said anything...not until Jared started to lead Annette away toward the cowgirl and cowboy lights.

"Just so you two know," Davis said, halting them, "we're not doing this to cause trouble for anyone."

Jared was still holding tight to Annette's hand.

"In fact," Davis said, "you'd be surprised to know that people in this town are more disposed to being friendly to you than you might think."

Jared's laugh was cutting. "There were a few ex-miners the other day who might disagree with you."

"They've been talked to, Jared," Davis said. "And you won't find them to be so disrespectful again."

Jared finally peered over his shoulder. "Why's that?"

"Let's just say that we're all trying to get along better these days."

Annette suspected that this new attitude in town had a lot to do with Davis, who'd been working for a long time to mend the rifts among the ex-miners, the so-called "richies" and everyone else who'd been caught in the middle of the social warfare after the kaolin mine closure had severely affected the town's economy more than five years ago.

Jared met Davis's gaze, paused for a second, then nodded to him.

"Thanks, Jackson," he said.

"No thanks necessary."

With a grin, Davis put his arm around his wife and led her into the cowgirl lights.

Annette watched them leave. "I think he likes you."

"I think he's still trying to get an interview and this is his new way of doing it."

She nudged him. "Don't you have any faith in humanity?"

He gave her a long look, and she could see a thousand different stories there—dark stories, like the day he'd visited his birth mom and the time he'd read that letter from his deceased dad revealing his adoption.

But then Jared's gaze gentled, and he cupped her face with one hand, running his thumb over her cheek.

"I'm getting more faith by the day," he said, bending down to kiss her right there in public.

Right where the lights surrounded them with so much hope and brightness.

Optimism was a strange thing.

As Jared drove back to Annette's condo that night, it got a hold of him as it never had before, maybe because of that meeting with Davis and Violet Jackson.

Or maybe because everything was starting to come together for Jared, and all it had taken was time…and the right woman.

When he took a detour on a side road in the opposite

direction of where they were supposed to be headed, Annette seemed bewildered.

"Are you lost?" she asked.

"No."

"Are you just plumb crazy then?"

"I guess I am." He smiled, steering onto a gravel driveway.

It didn't take long for the light from his cabin porch to appear over the slight hill.

As he pulled up to his rented home, Annette slid him a glance.

He said, "This is where I live."

"The Batcave?"

"Something like that."

From her seat, she inspected his domain: the aged pine plank walls, the windows that looked like an old man's dimmed, closing eyes.

"For a while," she said, "I thought maybe you didn't live anywhere."

"That's because I've never brought anyone here before."

The words meant more than they seemed. He wasn't just giving her a tour. He was ready to let her in.

Step by step, bit by bit, he was getting nearer to… He couldn't say what it was just yet, but it was becoming clearer every day. It was just a matter of when he'd be prepared to let her all the way into his life, with the darkest areas of himself bared.

She opened her truck door and got out before he could help her, as he always did. But that showed him, didn't it? Annette could handle herself.

She could handle a lot, if he would only give her the opportunity.

Climbing up the porch steps, she said, "I'm getting a real cabin-in-the-woods feeling but without the woods."

Around them, the moon swamped the long-bladed grass of a field, and he looked at it with a fresh gaze. The gaze Annette had given to him.

"I chose this place because it was off the beaten path," he said.

"Huge surprise." She smiled back at him from the porch as she waited by the doorway.

He hadn't locked up, so he opened the screen, allowing her to open the actual door and do the honors of going in first.

As she crossed his threshold, a thrill grabbed him. He'd never thought he would see the day when someone like Annette would be here, in a place he had only called his own.

But as soon as he hit the lights, she looked perfectly at home, standing amid the sparse furnishings that had come with this cabin—a Naugahyde sofa, two mismatched reclining chairs and a hickory end table holding a tacky lamp that someone had made out of a cowboy boot, probably as a joke. Behind her, the stone fireplace waited, and when she laid eyes on it, she took in a long breath.

"It's perfect," she said. "I always wanted a fireplace. They're so rustic."

He leaned against the wall, content to watch her. "What kind of houses are you used to?"

"Rented condos, just like the one I'm in now. My mom and I lived in hers for years before she died. Brett was going to buy it for me, but…"

"You wouldn't have been happy living in a place someone gave to you, Annie. If there's one thing I've learned about you, it's that you don't mind making your own way."

"I'd much rather do that than take scraps from someone like Brett." She went to the fireplace and ran her hand along the stone mantel. "I would've made a horrible trophy wife."

Jared wished he had more to give her than he did, even if she didn't want fancy trimmings and silver spoons.

She wandered over to a bookcase that was built into a wall. It was stacked with disorderly tomes bound by leather covers.

"Those belong to the owner, too," Jared said. "Lots of stuff with Greek names, but there're some art books, too."

She picked one up. It was huge, requiring her to hold it with both hands, and she brought it to the couch and let it thump to the cushion. Then she sat and gingerly opened it up.

"Oh," she said. "Impressionists. Monet. I used to try and paint like him during college until I found out that imitation really isn't the sincerest form of flattery if you stink at it."

"I'll bet your paintings were great."

"You would say that."

She grinned, and he automatically did, too, as if he were her puppet on a string—a place he didn't mind being.

"These really bring back some memories," she said, turning the page. "It seems like aeons ago that I wanted to pick up a paintbrush. It's like that kind of indulgence belongs in another person's life."

"You got pretty busy," he said, going over to the

couch and sitting, bracing his forearms on his thighs. "After everything settles down for you, you can go back to it."

"You know, I think I will."

Why was she smiling at him as if he was some sort of Valentine cupid who'd brought her a gift? He hadn't done anything but told her a fact—that she could do anything she set her mind to.

She was the strongest, most vital woman he knew, so why not?

When she closed the art book, he knew she had something on her mind again, and his stomach tightened.

"I've just been wondering…"

Uh-oh. This was how it always started out.

He waited, holding his breath.

"Tomorrow at nine," she said, "I'm going to the doctor for a checkup at the medical plaza in New Town."

Ah-ha. "You need a ride? It'd be no problem to give you one if you're going to be too tuckered out to drive."

"That's not exactly it, Jared."

So what was it?

She bit her lip, then said, "Dr. Andrews is giving me a sonogram, and I thought…well, maybe that you might want to come along?"

It was as if a fist had pounded him flat on the head, releasing images that he'd stowed away: his ex-wife showing him a picture of their unborn child and him taking it with him to the next rodeo. His little daughter in the arms of another man when Jared had seen the new family in a restaurant through a window, just before he'd walked away, knowing he had no right to invade their peace.

"I don't think that's a good idea," Jared heard himself saying now.

Annette didn't seem to understand. She knitted her eyebrows.

"I mean," Jared said, his voice flat, "I... God, I don't think it's my place to do that."

Her face paled.

Dammit, he hadn't meant to be so frank. But he hadn't expected her to ask such a thing, either, and so soon, at that.

Hadn't she been betrayed by a man not too long ago? How the hell had she bounced back so quickly?

How could she trust someone like him after what she'd gone through?

As she stood, pulling her coat around her as if shielding herself, Jared wanted to take it all back. It was just that she'd made things so damned real with that sonogram question when, these past hours, it'd seemed as if they were in a bubble that protected them from what was truly waiting outside.

Now that bubble had popped with one simple invitation.

"I didn't mean to say it like that," he told her, getting to his feet, too. "It's just..."

"It's just that I assumed too much." Her voice was as flat as his had been. "A few days together and I'm already asking you to do something a father should be doing. I'm sorry for putting you in such a weird place."

How could he tell her that he might've come around to doing something like this soon? That he was slowly but surely making progress and that she shouldn't lose faith in him?

See, Tony would've handled this better with the

woman he loved, Jared thought. Tony wouldn't have wasted a moment in saying yes to her.

"Annie..." he started.

But she was already going toward the door. "I'm really tired, Jared. Can you just take me home?"

This time, he had no choice but to say yes.

Annette could not believe she'd actually asked him to do such a thing.

Really? *Come to my sonogram with me?*

As she lay in bed that night, a drained glass of milk by her bedside and an herbal compress on her lower back, she wanted to beat her head against a wall.

She had no idea what had gotten into her, other than that asking him had seemed like a really good notion at the time. She'd just felt so close to Jared, what with them making love and then him taking her to his so-called cave. Both were big deals for a man like him, but she'd totally taken things too far.

And if she could tell anything from the mood in his truck on the ride over here, it was that she'd probably come off as a pushy, needy woman.

Which she wasn't.

Right?

She fell asleep wondering, though, then early the next morning, got ready and took off to get her sonogram, still wondering.

But things changed when, more than an hour and a half later, she was clutching a picture of her daughter in her hand.

A girl.

She rested a palm on her tummy as she walked through the parking lot. A little girl who would wear

pink dresses and want to have tea parties with her someday. A child who would hopefully resemble her birth
father in no way and who would nestle into her arms
dreaming sweet dreams every night.

The euphoria was enough to make Annette forget
what she'd done to Jared, but only for a short time, because when she got to her bright red car in the parking lot, she found a note waiting under the windshield
wiper.

She took it out, unfolding it.

*I knew you'd be here for your appointment, and
it wasn't hard to find your car. It stands out in
a crowd just like you do, Annie, and it was all I
could see. And that's why I'm not going to let another day go by without clearing the air with you.
Would you come over to my place tonight, 6:00?
I have some big apologies to make.*

It was signed by Jared.

She held the note for a few seconds while, in her
other hand, she grasped her daughter's ultrasound picture. It'd been the first one taken after Annette had finally decided to learn the sex of her baby, an important
moment to put in the scrapbook she planned to make
for her daughter.

It almost felt as if she was weighing the picture and
the note against each other.

Should she give Jared another chance, even if she
suspected that he was holding back from her when all
she wanted to do was rush into everything with him?

Or was she being too impulsive with a baby on the

way—a child who could get far more hurt than Annette had ever been by the betrayal of a man?

She slipped both papers into her coat pocket together, already knowing the answer.

When Jared heard Annette's car come up the graveled drive to park by his porch, his blood gave a mighty leap in his veins.

She'd left him a message on his cell earlier, while he'd been assuaging a fitful stallion at the ranch. And all day he'd been flying on adrenaline, counting the hours until he could see her again.

Her footsteps thudded on the porch, and she knocked on the door, the sound echoing his heartbeat.

Here went nothing.

When he answered, he had to take a moment, just as he did whenever he laid eyes on her. This time the porch light burnished her light blond hair, which she'd worn long and wavy. The lamp also lent a warm glow to her red coat and the cable-knit light blue sweater she wore over a plaid wool skirt. On her feet she was sporting those Ugg boots, as if they were the most comfortable thing a pregnant woman could wear.

He held the door open for her. "Glad you came, Annie."

Hope you make it worth my while, said her smile as she held out two items to him.

In one hand, she had a pie from the diner, packed in a box. In the other, Tony's journal.

He grasped on to both, then set the book on the nearby end table. The journal seemed to watch him, just as if Tony was here, encouraging him to be the best he could be.

"It's cherry pie," Annette said. "I know you like to have it on occasion."

"Thanks."

He stood aside, and she walked in, immediately becoming a part of his home again.

"You went in to the diner today?" he asked, taking her coat and draping it over a nearby flower-upholstered chair that didn't go with anything else in the room.

"Just for the pie. And to talk to Terry about modifying my work schedule."

He almost said it was high time for her to talk to her manager until he realized that he'd forfeited any right to be interested when he'd turned her down cold about the sonogram last night.

"How did Terry take it?" Jared asked instead.

"Great. He's going to have me work the register and do some of the accounting during slow times."

"I didn't know you were good at numbers."

"I'm okay. I took over my mom's finances when she got sick and I ran the household. Plus, I took a class in college, which impressed Terry for some reason."

Sometimes, when she sounded so responsible and together like this, it was easy to forget that she was only in her early twenties. Still, her eyes had seen a lot—of heartache and loss, betrayal.

When he noticed her gaze flick toward the fireplace, he suddenly remembered the dinner preparations and he made a beeline for it. He'd put aluminum-wrapped bundles in a tray over the fire, trying to impress her with his unusual cooking method.

"Foil dinners?" she asked, coming up beside him at the stone hearth. "I haven't had these since I was in Girl Scouts."

"I tried to make them the healthiest I could. I used ground turkey meat with vegetables. I also got some seven-grain bread and a cauliflower casserole from the market."

"You went to a lot of trouble."

"Not half as much as you deserve."

Her defenses seemed to melt right then and there, her shoulders sinking. "Are you trying to win me over or something?"

He turned to her. "I mean it, Annie. Last night was a bump in the road for us. I never intended to hurt you. I should've…"

"If you're about to say you should've said you'd go to the sonogram, don't. Yeah, it stung when you turned me down, but I was pushing things, Jared. I was in the moment, and I didn't stop to consider the big picture." She paused. "You'd think I would've learned to slow down after Brett. Lord knows I should've done my due diligence there."

"Annie," he said, coming closer to her, "you've got such a good heart. Never apologize for that."

They looked at each other, and he felt himself falling, fast and hard.

He wanted so badly to make her happy, even if he wasn't capable of it in the end.

"So how did your appointment go today?" he asked, smoothing a strand of hair back over her shoulder.

Her cheeks were pink, maybe because they were standing so close to the fire.

Maybe not, though.

"The appointment was a breeze," she said.

"Don't they give you pictures or something?"

After a moment of hesitation, she reached into

the pocket of her skirt, pulling out a carefully folded computer-generated picture.

Without a word, she showed it to him, and it was all Jared could do to swallow away the tightness in his throat.

He hadn't been sure just what a third-trimester baby would resemble, but it wasn't this—a definite child. The picture focused on the face, with the closed eyes and a thumb stuck in a cute little mouth.

"She's a girl," Annette said, her voice wavering.

A girl.

Just like the daughter he could've had if he'd held on to her.

The thought pummeled Jared, even as he touched the face on the picture, as if the baby could feel it.

Another little girl.

Another chance, he thought, keeping hold of the photo, unwilling to let it go.

Chapter Ten

Annette woke up the next morning in the most natural place possible—Jared's arms.

After eating last night, they had gone to his bed, fully clothed and intending only to lie down for a short time. She'd been tired from running around all day, and even though her sex drive had certainly been ready and willing, the rest of her had relaxed to the point of slumber. Jared had caressed her tummy, almost as if he was imagining the baby in the ultrasound photo beneath the bump and was lulling her to sleep, too.

Something had changed with Jared last night, and it seemed to have taken hold after he'd seen that picture. Not that Annette was complaining. It was nice cuddling up to him, feeling as if he could've been the father.

If only.

As he still slept now, she watched him. When he was

awake, his face was so often hard, his jaw gritted, as if he was always ready to fend off anything or anyone that confronted him.

But now?

Peaceful, she thought, using her fingertips to brush the dark five o'clock shadow on his cheek. A face a mother would've loved if his birth mom had given him half a chance.

But he had other people who loved him instead. She did, for instance. And Gran.

As Annette kept tracing the line of his jaw, her mind wandered, dwelling on every step Jared had taken to get where he was today.

The letter from his adoptive dad...the P.I. who'd told him about his birth mom and then his grandma...

And that was when something in her head clicked.

Gran was from his mother's side of the family. All of a sudden, it seemed like the most important detail in creation.

She brushed back his dark hair. "Jared?"

He stirred, moaning a little and bringing her closer to him.

Normally, she would have put talk by the wayside but not now.

"Wake up," she whispered.

He opened one eye. "Is everything okay?" Then he sat up. "Are you—"

"No, no, the baby and I are doing well." She sat up, too. "It's just that I thought of something important. Jeez, I can't believe I didn't ask you before."

He frowned.

"The day before yesterday," she said, "you told me

about how the P.I. you hired tracked down your living relatives here, and Gran was the only one."

"Okay…"

"Gran is your birth mom's mother. That means you already know who your great-grandma was, and she's most likely the woman Tony writes about in his journal. I can't believe I didn't zero in on that before." Didn't they say pregnant women could be scatterbrained? She might be living proof.

He started looking a little guilty.

"Jared?"

"I've had my suspicions about it."

For a speechless few seconds, she just sat there. Then she said, "Why didn't you say anything?"

"I didn't want to jump to any conclusions without Gran's input. And she won't give me any."

It was a lame excuse, and he seemed to know it.

"You didn't trust me with this particular secret," she said.

"Annie, I was getting around to it."

"Slowly." She couldn't help a note of frustration from creeping in. "Very, very slowly."

He gave her a loaded glance that told her he was still used to being the silent guy in black, but then he rested a hand on her arm.

"If you want to know, I'll tell you all about it."

Why now? Because she'd caught on and he had no other choice?

His hand trailed away from her. "When I first got to know Gran, she told me about our family. One of her stories was about my great-grandma Tessa Hadenfield. She was the daughter of the first sheriff of St. Valentine and her dad's pride and joy, basically because her mom died when she was young and she was all he had left."

"When did she meet Tony?"

"I have no idea. I've danced around the subject with Gran, but she always tells me he has nothing to do with our family."

"That has to be a fib. You've got Tony's looks, and we know Tessa's your great-grandmother. One plus one equals you."

"From what the journal says, we can assume that she and Tony got together before she married my great-grandfather Joseph." Jared drew up his knees, resting his forearms on them. "So I figure she must've passed her child off as his, unless my great-grandfather knew what was going on. Joseph and Tessa got married soon after Tony's death, according to what Davis and Violet Jackson have written in their articles."

"So if Tessa and Tony did have a child…"

"He'd be my granddad. Gran's husband, Richard."

"And he died before you could meet him. Have you seen pictures, just to compare your looks with him?"

Jared shrugged. "Sure, but my grandfather resembled Tessa, not Tony. I told you my birth mom doesn't look much like me, either, so I must've had some kind of recessive trait creep into me."

"Tessa was lucky that her son didn't look like Tony. It really saved her from having to give some hard explanations."

"Until I showed up years later."

"Well, she doesn't have to worry about that now."

He sent her a sheepish glance, and she wanted to ask him why it had been so damn hard to tell her about Tessa. It had seemed in the past that they were pretty good brainstorming partners when it came to working out his family tree.

Hadn't he noticed that they partnered well in every way? Or was he so used to working alone that the act of including someone else was too tough for him to handle?

She traced a seam on the quilt bunched under them as Jared measured her with his gaze.

"Do you feel better now?" he asked.

She nodded, even though the whole trustworthiness issue still lingered in the pit of her stomach.

Would she ever know all of Jared? Or would he always be revealing his life to her piece by piece, maybe even keeping things back until he had no other choice?

He got up from the bed, going to the hallway, and she thought the subject was closed. For now at least.

She sighed, reaching for her cell phone on a nightstand and checking her text messages. She'd heard a ding sometime during the night but had been too tuckered out to check her phone.

When she accessed her in-box, she found a short-but-sweet invitation from Violet Jackson for Rita Niles's baby shower in a couple of days.

Annette smiled, appreciating the gesture, even if it probably was an afterthought spurred by her recent meetings with Violet and Rita.

Jared came back in the room, and she put the phone down. He was holding Tony's journal, which was opened to a specific page.

"I want you to know that I can't have you losing faith in me, Annie."

It was the last thing she'd expected him to say.

"Thing is," he continued, "I'm not a man who's very

good with words, and it's hard for me to say stuff like that. Tony was good, though."

As he sat on the bed, he looked down at the journal, starting to read from one of the last pages.

"'I can only hope that they bury me next to her when the time comes,'" he said softly. "'She knows that, in life, all I wanted to show her was that she is my everything. Yes, it takes time to do that, and I do not know how much of that we have. But, just as I want to spend every moment with her while we live, I want an eternity beside her, too.'"

Jared shut the journal, and Annette held a hand out to him. He took it, connecting with her.

But the darkness was still in his eyes, even if he was doing his damnedest to chase it away.

She just about went weak with feelings for him. "I understand, Jared. Just like Tony, you need time to show me how you feel and who you are."

As Annette brushed her thumb over his, she knew that, no matter what, she was going to give him time enough to say in his own words everything Tony had said.

Luckily, unlike Tony and Tessa, they had all the time in the world.

The next two days passed with both of them working—Jared on the ranch and Annette at the cash register of the diner. At the end of their shifts, Jared would end up at her place, digging until he retired to her condo, where he'd bought her a bigger bed and moved the old one out.

"A thank-you gift for your thank-you gift," he'd told her when the bed had been delivered yesterday.

She'd clearly been tickled by his care and, in appreciation, they'd made good use of the gift.

Yup, things were smoother than ever between them. But how long was that going to last when he finally got up enough courage to come clean with her about everything in his past?

He'd almost told her about his daughter the other morning, when Annette had bristled at not knowing the truth about Tessa Hadenfield. But he'd decided that she was already too angry for him to add insult to injury, and he would sit her down and have a long talk soon.

Yet wasn't he always saying "soon"?

He dwelled over that question while he was in town today, rounding off his afternoon by picking up some fencing supplies from the mercantile.

But then he got a phone call that shook his schedule to bits.

It was Davis Jackson on the other end of the line, and after they got the hellos over with, Jared didn't even bother to ask the millionaire owner of the town paper how he'd gotten his number.

He was too stunned by what Davis had to say.

"Do you have any free time?" he asked Jared. "And I'm not angling for an interview. I need to talk with you about something Vi and I found out."

If a bolt of lightning had hit Jared, it wouldn't have rocked him any more than this.

News. They had uncovered something about Tony, hadn't they?

Even though Jared had been digging for his own answers, a sense of dread raked through him.

"I've got some time," he said warily, "and I'm in town."

"Good. Vi is at Rita Niles's baby shower, but I'm at the newspaper office."

Jared remembered Annette had been planning to go to the party, too. "I'll be there in a few."

He hung up, leaning against the tailgate of his truck, which he'd just shut after loading the fencing supplies.

Davis's tone had set Jared on edge. It had sounded like a prelude to bad news, and on the screen of his mind, he saw his image of wonderful town founder Tony Amati crumbling.

But Jared wasn't going to find out a thing by standing around, so he headed for the newspaper office just off the boardwalk, past Whitefeather's Jewelry Boutique.

When he walked in, Davis, who'd dressed down today in a casual Western shirt with jeans, was huddled over one of the computer desks.

When Davis saw him, he said, "Thanks for coming," and gestured to a chair.

As Jared sat down, Davis handed over a computer-generated grainy black-and-white picture.

"This is from an old newspaper," he said, "circa late 1920s Chicago."

Jared scanned the photo. A man was in the foreground, his arm propped on a railing in some sort of office. He was smiling, his slicked dark hair parted on the side, his chin emphasized by a dimple. He'd taken off his suit jacket, revealing a long-sleeved white shirt, a black tie with tiny designs that Jared couldn't make out and a vest. He had his arm around a random man in a suit, the guy's face halfway cut off by the camera.

"Who is he?" Jared asked, focusing on the main subject. "And what does he have to do with Tony?"

Davis leaned back in his chair. "That's George Moran. His nickname was 'Bugs.'"

Who?

The reporter continued. "They say Moran ran liquor during Prohibition and was set up by Al Capone to take the fall for the execution of his own men during a massacre in his warehouse. Seven guys were killed that day by hired assassins who were pretending to be cops on a raid. They were supposed to get Moran because he was a rival in the booze business with Capone, but Bugs wasn't there. You've probably heard about this slaughter by its more famous name."

Jared shook his head.

"The St. Valentine's Day Massacre," Davis said.

St. Valentine's Day Massacre.

St.…Valentine?

Jared's gaze went fuzzy as he forced his attention to the man next to Bugs Moran in the picture.

Only half a face, but now that Jared looked more carefully, beyond the greased hair and the fancy suit…

No.

It had to be someone else. Not Tony.

But then the name of this town suddenly took on new, awful meaning for Jared, and he tried to deny what was already locking together in his mind.

"Hey," Davis said, sitting on the edge of his chair, "we've got a lot more research to do, and we don't know exactly what Tony might've had in common with the massacre or with Bugs. We found this picture in a whole batch of archived Chicago newspaper photos from Tony's era, but the second we identified him—"

"We don't know that it *is* him," Jared said.

Davis took a second, then said, "Now that we have a

lead, we've been able to isolate other pictures of Bugs and his cohorts. It seems that Tony's in a few of those photos."

After extracting more printouts from a manila folder, Davis pushed them on the desk toward Jared.

He didn't look at them, though, because none of this could be true.

The St. Valentine's Day Massacre? Al Capone?

It had to be a fever dream conjured up by two reporters who wanted to make a buck for this town by creating a whale of a tale. And what a story it was.

But the big hole in the entire narrative was that Tony was a *good* man. He had founded this town and had helped families get back on their feet with the money he'd made from oil. He had been a revered presence whose only faults were that he liked his privacy and he'd secretly fallen in love with a woman who was soon to be married to another man.

Then an unwelcome detail wormed its way into Jared's mind. Tony had referred time and again in his journal to escaping some kind of past.

He felt fragmented, as if the identity he'd craved, based on his new family, had begun sifting apart, just like the beginning of an avalanche.

"Jared?"

He finally registered Davis's voice, and it seemed as if he'd been saying his name more than once.

Jared set the first picture down on the desk, and it covered all the others as Davis spoke.

"Violet and I wanted to talk to you before we pursued this...or published anything."

"There won't be anything to publish about Bugs and

this—" Jared indicated the pictures "—this other man who's not Tony."

Davis offered the other photos again. "Look, it's true that we haven't absolutely confirmed the identity of the guy in the pictures with Bugs yet, but…"

On a burst of doubt, Jared grabbed the other pictures that Davis had wanted him to look at. Much to his relief, none of them had a clear picture of Tony.

"These mean nothing," he said, pushing them away. "The only thing you have on Tony are the stories you already know, all of them saying that he was an upstanding citizen."

"Jared—"

He came close to telling Davis about Tony's journal, which would prove his probable great-grandfather was a decent man deep down, no matter what.

But that would be desperate, and even if there was a small, wailing part of Jared that threatened to believe the worst about Tony, he wouldn't expose his innermost thoughts to a reporter, not for any reason.

The other morning he'd realized that Annette was the only person he'd trusted, ever. And when he told her about this…

Maybe she'd calm him down, as she always did.

He got up from his chair. "I appreciate your wanting to let me in on this, but it wasn't necessary."

"We're not stopping the investigation," Davis said.

Panic jarred him, but what was he going to do? Plead with Davis to leave well enough alone? Beg him to preserve what might be a fantasy about Tony and all the hopes Jared had pinned on him?

"You do what you need to do for this town," Jared

said, going toward the door. "But I guarantee you'll come to another dead end with this latest lead."

As he exited, he thought about Annette again. She would put this all into perspective. She would know that Tony couldn't possibly be what it seemed like he might've been—a criminal.

A black hat.

"You're getting close...closer..." said the baby shower guests in the St. Valentine Hotel's tearoom.

Rita Niles's cowgirl sister, Kim, was blindfolded by a pink bandanna decorated with images of a chubby-cheeked infant girl. Meanwhile, she grasped a cutout picture of a baby with tape on the back, and her hands were outstretched as she clumsily searched for the fake tummy propped in a chair in a game of "Place the Baby on the Mommy."

It was a version of "Pin the Tail on the Donkey," and Annette was so very happy that no one had thrown her a shower and foisted games like these on her friends.

Then again, Violet Jackson, Rita's best friend, had gotten an early start on shower-throwing because some of Conn's and Rita's family members were in town for their wedding this weekend. And, Annette reminded herself, there was still plenty of time for some soul to put together a baby extravaganza before her delivery date.

"You're getting warm, Kim!" shouted Margery Wilmore, one of Rita's older hotel employees.

Kim was actually on a collision course with Conn's mother, who sat in a chair by the gift table, stifling a laugh. Nearby, Rita watched with amusement as her sister stumbled about in her denim skirt and cowboy boots.

Next to Rita, Violet Jackson sat quietly. Every once in a while, she would give Annette a strange glance, and Annette had no idea why. It was as if the woman were nervous about something.

But why would that be if she'd been friendly enough to invite Annette to this shower?

In the end, Kim taped the baby picture to Conn's mom. The women cheered for the cowgirl, probably just because she'd managed to get through her turn.

"I give up," Kim said after ripping off her blindfold. "This is such a ridiculous game."

Rita laughed. "I'd like to hear you say that during your own shower someday."

"Don't count on one of those," Kim said, handing the blindfold off to Violet's mother, Andrea. "Here, Mrs. Osborne, have at it."

"I'd like to go last," said the woman with gray-sprinkled red hair. "It's part of my strategy."

No-nonsense Kim gave the blindfold to Annette, who was sitting next to Andrea Osborne, then took her own seat again, seemingly bored out of her mind.

Annette got up, ready to put on the bandanna.

"Wait," Rita said. "I think Annette should sit this one out. I don't love the idea of spinning around a woman who's even more pregnant than I am and then expecting her to trip around blindfolded."

Everyone agreed, and Annette didn't mind so much.

As she handed off the bandanna to Margery, the matronly woman said, "So have you and Jared thought of a name for your child yet?"

Boing. That was what it sounded like as Margery's faux pas bounced through the room.

No time like the present to set everyone straight. "This isn't actually Jared's baby," Annette said.

She felt kind of funny explaining this to a roomful of women she didn't know very well, but what else could she do?

Rita took up her cause. "Annette was pregnant when she got to St. Valentine."

"That's right," Margery said, thumping herself on the head. "I'd heard your husband passed away. I'm sorry about that."

Annette didn't correct her. "Thank you."

"It does seem," Margery said, "that you have a ready-made father handy, though. Doesn't it?"

"Margery," everyone said at the same time.

Annette had heard that the woman didn't have many boundaries when it came to sticking her nose in everyone's business. Heck, maybe this was just some sort of St. Valentine initiation that she'd have to endure to be accepted.

"It's all right," Annette said, sitting down and hoping everyone would get back to the game pronto.

And they did, with Margery taking her turn.

Blindfolded and obviously disoriented, Margery immediately headed the wrong way, toward the exit to the tearoom, and the ladies hooted. Annette sat there, quietly circling her palm over her belly.

Obviously, it was quite natural for people in this town to think Jared was the father. It seemed as if the rumor that had circulated recently hadn't died out.

At the very thought, something between a jabbing ache and a contented glow filled Annette. She only wished this little girl were Jared's child and that everything between her and him was as perfect as the towns-folk apparently believed.

But even after Annette had gotten on Jared for avoiding the truth about Tessa Hadenfield with her, she couldn't shake the feeling that he was still acting like a stranger in some ways.

She hated that, though, because truly, she did want to believe in him.

Margery was just making her way back to the chairs when, behind her, the door to the hallway opened.

As Jared appeared, Annette sat up in her chair, charged by seeing him. But something about his expression gave her pause.

And something about the way Violet Jackson had gone stiff in her chair.

Without interrupting, he made it clear that he'd like to see Annette, so she glanced at Rita.

She smiled, gesturing for Annette to go to him.

Violet merely watched Jared, as if inspecting him. As if wondering if he was okay.

Why did Annette get that feeling?

She grabbed her purse, and after he'd shut the door behind her, she rested her free hand on his forearm.

"What's wrong?" she asked.

"I hate to pull you out of there, Annie, but I've got something to tell you."

It sounded urgent, and she went with him into the falling evening, where he led her toward his truck parked on Amati Street.

He helped her into the cab, then drove.

"Jared," she said, "you're scaring me."

"I don't mean to. But this is a discussion that needs some privacy."

"What's it about?"

They had come to the edge of town, and he pulled under an oak tree near Piell's Gas Station, where a vintage Phillips 66 sign accompanied another one that said Pumps Are Closed.

After turning off the ignition, Jared wiped a hand over the lower half of his face. She saw that he was tired.

So very tired.

"Davis Jackson pulled me into his office today," he said.

Annette unbuckled her seat belt so she could slide closer to Jared on the seat.

"And?"

"And he told me something that shocked the tar out of me."

He described a picture he'd seen of a Prohibition-era liquor runner named Bugs Moran with his arm around a man whose face was only partially visible.

"Davis told me that he and Violet think the other guy in the picture is Tony," Jared said.

His voice was flat again, just as it always got when he shut down. But Annette wasn't going to let that happen.

"Do you have the picture with you?" she asked.

"I bolted out of that office so fast that I didn't think to grab it."

At least she knew now why Violet had been so odd toward her at the shower. "So what do you think? Did it look like Tony?"

"Yes." The answer seemed bitter in Jared's mouth.

She allowed the information to sink in, but it didn't seem real.

"What does this mean then?" she asked.

"It means that Davis and Violet are going to investigate further."

She touched his hand on the steering wheel. "You're afraid that Tony won't be the man you wish he was."

"I know who he was. His journal shows me who he was."

Even Annette could tell that Jared was clinging to his last hopes about Tony—that his so-called mirror was cracking and his fanciful perception of his great-grandfather was damaged.

Maybe along with his own self-image.

"Do you really think," she asked, "that anything you find out about Tony is going to matter? Especially to me?"

He barely nodded, staring straight ahead.

She wouldn't let him distance himself like this, so she put her hand under his chin and turned his gaze to her. It was dark with banked anger, helpless fury... and despair.

"Jared, I already know what I think of you, and it's all good. It's pure. And it's enough for me to want you to be in my life and my baby's life forever."

Her confession rang in the cab, and he shut his eyes.

"Did you hear what I said?" She didn't mean to, but she grasped his chin harder. "You're the man I want to raise my daughter."

A swell of emotion seemed to take him over as he opened his eyes.

So dark, so confused...

"Annie," he said, his voice shaking, "I already have a daughter."

Chapter Eleven

Jared had known that Annette would look just like this when he told her.

Destroyed. Puzzled beyond measure.

Betrayed.

It was unfortunate that the truth had come out in this way, but it was too late to go back now. Too late for so many things because he couldn't change history—not Tony's, not his.

"A daughter?" she finally asked, her voice just a creak.

Then it all came out of him—the avalanche that had started when he'd heard about gangster Tony, the pain that had been threatening to spill.

"That ex-wife I told you about," he said. "She's the mother of my daughter, Melissa. Joelle and I got married too soon after meeting each other. I'd left home recently, running away from my uncle Stuart's ranch after I'd read that letter about my adoption. You could say I was myopic, focusing on what I'd always wanted to do—bust broncs on the rodeo circuit."

He tried to lock his gaze to Annette's, but this time she was the one who wouldn't meet his eyes.

Still, he went ahead. "I was reeling, but I found a home on the circuit. Nobody bothered me much about where I'd been or where I was going, yet I felt like there were so many others like me there. We were an odd family, and that filled a void. So did the adrenaline rush I got from competing."

"A rush," she said, as if she had to utter something, so it might as well be this.

"Yeah. A rush. See, for a long time I'd suffered from my parents' deaths, and I needed... Well, I didn't know what I needed back then. Uncle Stuart had always done his best to make me feel at home on his ranch, but he'd never gotten married, never had kids or been a part of any significant relationships. He liked being alone, and I felt that about him. So when I found out I was adopted, it made me feel more isolated than ever, and it wasn't too hard to leave."

"So you could find what you needed."

Part of him argued that he shouldn't be searching Annette's face for more of a response, that he should be as removed as possible, because it had always worked in the past.

But it didn't feel right. Not with Annette.

"I ended up at the rodeo, like I wanted." He was still gripping the steering wheel, and he let up on it. "I met Joelle after a rodeo one night. She was a buckle bunny but not in a way that meant she slept around. She was looking for love. I suppose I was, too, in a way, and I told myself that I'd found it with her. But I was actually just too selfish to know what I was talking about. At any rate, she got pregnant right away, and when she told me the news, I came out of my dream world and realized that it was too soon for me to take care of anyone—a wife...a child."

"And how long ago was this?" Annette asked.

"About twelve years now."

The moonlight was starting to invade the inside of the truck through the windshield, and it didn't offer its usual gleam. Instead, it made Annette look pale.

Jared's heart stirred, as if trying to tell him something, but the careful part of him pushed it away.

"So you were only twenty-one when this happened." At this, Annette's gaze seemed to give off a little spark of optimism. "You were young."

"You're about the same age as I was, and I can't imagine you being the same way."

And there went the flash of hope he'd seen in her. Gone. Just like that.

He went on. "Joelle had no idea what was going through my head. I shut her out. So when she asked me to leave the rodeo—she said it was too dangerous for a daddy—I refused."

"Why?"

"Because the feeling of winning and being admired was the only thing filling the void."

She was touching her belly now, as if wondering if he'd been pretending for a time that he'd enjoyed the feel of *this* baby and that he was going to drop her cold, as he had with his other one.

At least she understood what he was. What he always might be.

"That's when my wife left me," he said, wishing he didn't want to touch Annette and her baby now. "She told me I wasn't father material. I knew she was right, too. After that, I went on the road again, sending home child support and writing letters, thinking I would somehow change my mind. Then I heard that she'd fallen for a cowboy who did take it upon himself to retire from the rodeo to be with her and Melissa. That's when I knew without a doubt that she and the baby would be much better off without me."

Annette was shaking her head, but she wasn't saying anything. It was as if she were fending off every word.

"I know in my soul," he said, "that the man Melissa calls Father is the best thing that happened to her and Joelle."

"But she's yours, Jared. How can you..."

"Just leave her like that?"

He sent a laden glance to her. *Look who I am. Did you expect any different?*

"You can't compare yourself to your birth mom," Annette said. "You hadn't even met her yet."

"Then I'd say it's in the blood."

Bad blood, and it might have traveled on down the line, from Tony Amati, to his birth mom, to him.

But he didn't want to believe it—about Tony or him.

You couldn't run from the truth, though....

Annette had inched away from him, and he hadn't even noticed until the space between them became obvious, like a wound that was starting to bleed.

"So that's it?" she asked.

"What more is there? Several years later, I had to retire from the rodeo after I got too old to be competitive at bronc busting." And that's when he'd felt the void more keenly than ever.

That's when he'd also regretted his treatment of Melissa more than he'd thought possible. He'd even hoped that she wouldn't ever think of him.

"You never went back to your daughter," Annette repeated, as if she was finally accepting who he was.

"I wasn't about to ruin a good family. That would've made me an even worse person because Melissa should've been free to love her adoptive dad the way I remember loving the man and woman I called my real parents."

Annette remained silent, and Jared knew he'd lost.

That he *was* lost, more than ever, without her.

He hurt all over—his chest, especially, where he'd dug his own heart out.

"After that," he said, needing to finish this, "my uncle Stuart died. He left me his ranch, and I decided to sell it. And he would've understood that I couldn't be tied down. The ranch was on the slide anyway, and he'd been looking to get out of the life himself." Jared swallowed, remembering how hard his uncle had attempted to be a decent parent, even though he wasn't made of the right stuff for it. But at least he'd tried. "That's when I hired the P.I. to track down my birth mom. The loneliness got to me, I guess. And the curiosity."

Now Annette's voice was hard. "And that's when you realized that it'd probably be safer to be a drifter, right? It'd be easier to distance yourself from everyone else before they could do it to you."

She'd hit the target, and the punch reverberated through him. He wanted to tell her that, even as he drifted, there was always a place in him that longed for some roots and an identity.

But she already knew that.

And it wouldn't matter.

She only proved his worst fears when she opened the truck's door and got out.

"Annie—"

But she was already walking down the road, back toward town.

He followed and caught up to her in a heartbeat. "Where do you think you're going?"

She whirled around, firing back with her own question. "What were you doing with me then? Were you trying to make up for all your mistakes? Being a constant boyfriend, being someone I thought could make a great dad?"

He'd asked himself that before. What had he been doing?

And why, now as he stood on a deserted road with Annette, did it seem as if he'd had the ability to be good at both?

"You know what the final blow is, Jared?" Annette had her arms crossed over her chest, as if a chill had taken her over. "It's the fact that you still kept this detail from me, even after I told you that I could handle everything you could throw my way. Even after you read from Tony's journal to me."

The journal. It was the one thing that Jared knew was true—just as true as the words he'd spoken to her.

Just as true as the man he'd wanted to be.

"How many more secrets do you have?" Annette

asked, her voice bruised. "And what kind of damage are they going to cause?"

"I don't have anything left to hide," he said, but it sounded so damned hollow.

Because he was that way now. Empty as a shell.

As she began walking back to the truck, he knew more than he'd ever known anything that he loved her. But what was the point in saying it now, when he'd already lost her?

Before she opened the driver's side door, she said one more thing to him.

"I wish you could see yourself as I do, Jared. You break my heart every time you refuse to look at what *I* can see so clearly."

He let her climb into the cab, turn the keys that he'd left in the ignition and take off without him, even though all the fencing equipment he'd bought at the mercantile was still in the back.

Was she so angry at him that she wasn't thinking straight? He let her go, hardly blaming her.

Making his way back to town, he got his cell phone out of his pocket so he could call the ranch for a ride. But as he reached for his cell, his hand brushed the pocket watch Annette had given him as a thank-you gift.

Just like a watch Tony would've worn.

He held it in his hand as he stopped walking, seeing Annette's face in the shine of the cover, seeing her smile.

Seeing what could've been.

Annette couldn't feel a thing.

As she parked Jared's truck outside her condo, she

barely remembered even driving there because she'd been in such a clouded, numbed state.

It wasn't so much that Jared had a sordid past—he obviously had been tearing himself up about it for years, and she knew without a doubt that he had it in him to redeem himself. It was that he didn't have enough faith in her to stay by his side as he dealt with his problems.

Didn't he know that she was stronger than that?

Hadn't she grown up a lot herself during the past several months?

She knew that she had, but it was sad that Jared hadn't noticed. Or that he didn't care to.

She got out of the truck, easing to the ground, and once she had locked it, she stared at the keys dangling from her hand.

A tremble rumbled in the middle of her chest. Was it…laughter? Heck, why not? She had stolen Jared's truck and left him stranded beside the road near town. She had ditched a baby shower like some madcap idiot and would have to apologize to Rita for not coming back.

It was all so ridiculous. It was…

As the laughter shook her, it turned to tears—great, racking sobs that forced her to lean against the truck, crying her heart out.

She loved him, and it tore her apart to not be loved back.

Was it that hard for someone to treasure her as her mom had treasured her dad? What was wrong with her that she kept being thrown back into the single-girl pond?

She didn't know how long she cried, but by the time she was done, her head had unclouded slightly, and she brought out her disposable phone to send a quick, efficient text message to Jared.

Your keys are under my front doormat.

And that was all. Half of her wanted to say sorry for snaking his truck, but he was the one who should be apologizing, not her.

Even so, she hoped that he was safe. It wasn't as if St. Valentine was crime-ridden or frightening at night, and Jared could handle himself, but...

She dropped the thought, heading for her condo. It took her longer than she thought to get there, though, because a neighbor stopped her under the glow of a walkway lamp.

"Evening, Annette," said Mr. Bandy, who lived a couple condos down. He was a bank loan officer in New Town who favored checkered sweater vests, Dockers and loafers.

"Hi, Mr. Bandy." She resisted the temptation to wipe at her eyes. They were swollen from crying, so why bring attention to that?

He seemed not to notice. "Big plans for Valentine's Day tomorrow?"

Oh, wow. How had she forgotten?

Her chest constricted. "I'm just having a quiet night in," she said.

"I thought you and your boyfriend might be having some kind of romantic dinner, then digging up more of the land out back. What're you looking for anyway?"

She'd had a feeling that neighbors had been talking about Jared's out-of-the-ordinary activity, and there was no reason to lie about it. "He's on an artifact hunt of sorts. This used to be Tony Amati's ranch, so he thought—"

"A history buff," Mr. Bandy said. "Say no more. He's sure devoted, though, isn't he? But why not, when he's the spitting image of Tony?"

Mr. Bandy said good-night, and Annette watched him go back to his condo. Talking about Jared had made things worse instead of better. Would it always be that way?

She wandered toward her door, shutting off her phone and going inside to a lonely home.

It was a long night, full of tossing and turning, and when she woke up in the late morning, after sleeping in, the first thing she checked while still dressed in the oversize sweater and sweatpants she'd slept in was her welcome mat outside the door.

The truck keys were gone.

Annette slowly closed the door. Jared hadn't used his spare key to come in. Did that mean she'd pushed him away for good?

But then she remembered her phone, and she turned it on.

When it dinged, she checked her in-box. There was a text from Jared.

Her breathing quickened when she saw other texts come through, indicating how long the message was.

Last night, I almost let myself in with the spare key you gave me, but I couldn't bring myself to. I figure you'll let me know when it's fitting for me to see you again, so I can tell you what a mistake I made when I let you go. I should've chased you down. I don't want to let you go, Annie.

She sank against the inside door frame, needing something to hold her up. Her knees had gone rubbery, her throat tender and raw.

At least some time alone gave me an opportunity to put my thoughts together. My own thoughts this time, not Tony's, and not from anyone else's journal.

For so long, I never thought much of myself. Maybe I'm wrong about that, though, because I recall being happy as a kid, when my parents were around. It was after they died, when I was already at the lowest I could be, that I found the letter about the adoption. That's no excuse for what I've done to my daughter and to you and the baby, Annie, but I needed to say it now, while I can.

I hope I've been clear with you, because I can't live without you—and it isn't just because I'm trying to make up for the way I treated my daughter. Tony never was clear with the woman he loved. I don't want to run out of time like it seems he did.

I want you in my life, Annie. I want your little girl in it, too. It's up to you as to whether you'll have me.

She kept the phone out, even as the glow of the screen dimmed. It was up to her, he'd said.

Did she trust him enough for *her* to stay? Or would she be another runaway would-be bride?

The sound of her doorbell clanged through her, and she started. Her heart was in her throat.

She was so excited, believing that Jared had come

back, that she didn't look through the peephole, and she opened the door, her smile taking her over.

But when she saw who it was, her breath caught in her chest, tightening, choking.

She tried to close the door, but before she could, he stopped her.

"Don't, Annette," he said, pushing it open. "You've got to let me in."

She gripped her phone, paralyzed by fear as she looked into Brett Cresswell's eyes.

After Jared had sent the text to Annette last night, he'd slept with the phone by his bed.

He couldn't really call it "sleeping," though, because he hadn't gotten in a damned wink. And when she hadn't returned the message, he had forced himself to go about his business this morning, not caring if it was Valentine's Day, not caring that he had the day off and could spend it however he wanted to.

He only yearned to be with her, coddling her and the baby, showing her that he was going to be a changed man.

His own man.

At least, that was how he'd started off the day, showering, preparing to find something to do with himself while he waited for a sign from Annette.

When he'd gotten a phone call, he'd jumped at it.

But it hadn't been Annette on the other end.

"Jared," said Davis Jackson.

It was right then that Jared knew something big was going down, so Jared had gone to the newspaper office again. This time, though, Violet was there with her husband.

What they had told Jared this morning was enough to send him straight over to Gran's house, where he knocked on the door and waited for her to answer.

When she did, she apparently realized there was something amiss, and she invited him in to her family room and to sit on the same couch he'd sat on all those times he'd asked her about his roots.

He hunched over, his hat next to him on the cushion as he peered up at the delicate old woman on the chair nearby, her hands gripping the armrests.

"Tony's name was really Sean Mullaney," Jared said. "He wasn't even Italian, even though he could pass for it. He was Irish, and he changed his name and heritage when he came out West because he had to. Then again, you knew that, didn't you, Gran?"

She hesitated, then nodded.

He let out a long breath.

"Don't be disappointed in me, Jared," she said. "The family always promised never to let the truth out of our family."

"And I'm not part of your family?"

"Don't say that." She raised her finger. "The moment I saw you on my doorstep, looking so much like Tony, I realized that this was it—the time we'd all been fearing—and I was the only person left to stand for what pride my husband had in his family until his dying day. I had hoped you would just drop all those questions you had about Tony, and I thought you eventually would. You kept saying you weren't sticking around here for very long."

"So you wondered why I should know everything if it seemed that I wasn't really going to be a part of the family?"

"Yes, that's what I thought at the time."

He girded himself for the answer to his next question. "If I'd have told you that I wanted to stay around St. Valentine, would you have told me all about Tony?"

"I would've gotten around to it. But maybe I'm a lot like you—lacking in the trust other people come by so easily."

His birth mom had done a lot of damage to both of them—he was sure of it. She'd taught them to be extra careful, to always guard yourself, no matter how much you wanted to be a part of someone, as Gran no doubt genuinely did with him.

He just hadn't given her much reason to.

"Then can we set things to rights now?" he asked.

She gave him a weighted glance, and he added, "Family's honor, Gran. I already know more than you wanted me to, and I won't say a word to the reporters about anything you tell me."

She took his promise seriously. "Understand, Jared, that we were protecting Tessa *and* Tony. She was on her deathbed when she revealed the truth to my husband, her son, and made him promise to keep it to ourselves. She only wanted to relieve her soul before she passed— and she wanted my Richard to know about his real father. She believed Tony was the best of men, even if she found out the truth about him on the night he died."

Something Annette had said to Jared last night haunted him. *How many more secrets do you have? And what kind of damage are they going to cause?*

Come to find out that Tony's secrets had caused plenty in the end.

Good God, why hadn't Annette returned his text? He wanted to tell her he understood now, that he wanted to get on with their life before fate took it away, just as it obviously had with Tony and Tessa.

But he hadn't heard a word from her yet.

Would he ever?

Gran had started to talk again. "From what Tessa told your grandfather, Tony really had been a Texas Ranger. He used to entertain Tessa with his adventures on the border, and she used to think of him as such a hero. At the end of his career, he was wounded by a bullet, and he eventually found himself without a job or a badge. It was the late twenties, and like a lot of others, he went to the big city looking for work."

"Chicago," Jared said. Davis and Violet had confirmed as much today, based on what they'd found out by contacting some historians and interviewing descendants of a few main players in this story. "Tony got caught up with Bugs Moran and liquor running."

"Tessa said he ran liquor because he needed the money for a sick mother."

Jared waited until Gran met his gaze again. "Davis and Violet told me about the St. Valentine's Day Massacre, too. They got a hold of a hidden eyewitness account that said Tony was definitely one of the men in that warehouse, but he made it out before the bullets started flying."

Until someone had ended up killing Tony in *this* St. Valentine.

Jared was at the point where the story didn't do much of anything to him anymore. The numbness of knowing that Tony wasn't a hero at all had settled in like shrapnel that had hit him hard and buried itself near his heart.

Now there were just more questions, and one of them kept dogging Jared.

In spite of the promises he'd made to Annette, *would* he revert back to his lineage? Would all the bad blood he had come boiling up again?

Gran wouldn't know that, though.

"I don't get why Tony would name this town after something that almost killed him," he said, getting back on track.

Gran shrugged. "Tessa said that Tony had a wild streak. He hid it well after he bought land and struck oil down here and became Mr. Respectable, but it was there. You could say he was even hiding in plain sight, and a perverse side of him was daring anyone who knew that he'd gotten away to come and find him on his own terms and his own territory. He was cocky with a gun, being a former Ranger. He didn't have much fear, and he probably never dreamed that it would turn out the way it did after he met Tessa."

"The sheriff's daughter."

"Yes. I don't think he ever thought he'd fall in love at all, much less with the daughter of a lawman. He was planning on spending his life in solitude. But then they saw each other at the spring picnic, after the sheriff was hired on."

Jared could imagine how Tony had felt. He had been the same when we he had spotted Annette working at the diner on the day that had changed his life.

He thought of Tony's journal entries, his confessions of "terrible sins." He knew what those were now, but it really hit hard because, like Jared, Tony had a woman who'd brought him out of his darkness.

Wasn't there hope for Jared then?

"All along," Jared said, "I knew Tessa was the woman in Tony's journal. After a time, Davis and Violet seriously suspected it, too, but they didn't want to publish it without confirmation."

When they'd told Jared this, he had been stunned that they'd kept it a secret. Yet the reporters were pros for a reason: they'd taken Jared's resemblance to Tony and put it together with Gran's heritage and wanted proof before going public.

How long would it take everyone else in town to shout out the obvious? Surely a lot of others would suspect it, too, just as soon as more people caught wind that Jared had a maternal grandma just out of St. Valentine.

Gran said, "Outside of a DNA test from you, how will the Jacksons have enough proof to run a story about Tessa and Tony?"

"They're debating what to do from this point on, but I think they truly want Tony to remain a good guy. At least, I'm hoping so."

"Well, that's a blessing because a day did come when Tony was found by Capone's men. Al never liked his strings to be left loose."

This was the reason Jared had come to Gran. Davis and Violet hadn't known the details of Tony's death, and he held his breath, hoping, praying that he would hear something that would give him a reason to think people could change.

That Tony had lived up to every word of that journal.

"Two hired killers came to town," Gran said. "They blended in, identifying Tony as Sean Mullaney, watching his daily routines, noticing that he couldn't keep his gaze off the sheriff's daughter when she strolled down the boardwalk with her friends.

"Tony made them, though, but just before he confronted them, one of the assassins sneaked into the

Hadenfield house, taking Tessa hostage and calling for Tony to surrender so they could wrap up one of Al's 'loose ends.' He'd been jailed for income tax evasion by then, but that didn't stop him from giving orders from his cell."

Jared couldn't move. "They threatened her?"

"At gunpoint. And they told her all about the 'Irish pig' and his past, just to degrade Tony. She was made of steel, though, and she didn't break. She yelled at Tony to run away, but he didn't."

Something blipped within Jared. Hope?

Gran smiled, tears in her eyes. "He went into that house and tried to save her, but they got him first. He died in front of Tessa just as the sheriff barged in with his deputy and took the killers out."

It was as if something burst inside of Jared, and he pushed back at his own pulsing emotions.

Gran said, "The sheriff's office whitewashed the entire incident, calling it a break-in. That's what the papers reported. And when it became obvious that Tessa was pregnant, he sped up her engagement to her fiancé. Joseph was a good friend of the sheriff's, older, a widower, and they passed off Tessa and Tony's son, your grandfather, as their own. It turned out that her husband couldn't have children, so he raised Richard with a lot of love."

Jared thought of Tony's last request in his journal, which must've ended just before the killers had come to town.

Bury me next to her...

"Where is Tony really buried, Gran?"

"I had told you it might be up at Heartbreak Hill, but no one truly knows. The sheriff had cleaned up

Tony's house right afterward, taking Tony's body and then finding an undisclosed resting place. He wouldn't tell Tessa any more than that about it. He wanted her to forget Tony."

Jared's heart cracked. So his great-grandfather and great-grandmother *were* apart, even in death. It left a dark spot on him, right alongside the one that still remained there—the one he'd earned by leaving his daughter.

But couldn't both of them be erased, just as Tony had erased his own?

Gran's gaze pleaded with him. "I'm dead serious about keeping this in the family, Jared. It would've shamed your grandfather if anyone had known the truth."

"But I'm the truth." He gestured to himself. "There's no denying it now. Tony's always going to be a part of our history. St. Valentine already knows I belong to your family, Gran, and they can keep suspecting I'm related to Tony all they want. But there's nothing that says I need to give them all the details. Just the fact that I know where I come from makes all the difference."

Her eyes went teary again and, for the first time, Jared went to his grandma for a hug. She embraced him wholeheartedly, telling him that he would never lack for a home.

But, in all this, the one thing he realized above all others was that he wanted to give Annette a home, too.

When Gran went to the kitchen to put together lunch, he gathered his guts to finally call the woman he would do anything for, even if she wasn't going to call him.

But when Annette answered the phone, all Jared

heard on the other end of the line was a clatter, then a male voice.

"Did you really think I wouldn't notice you were gone, Annette?"

Stunned, he listened for another few seconds, as the mystery man kept talking, hardly sounding like a friend of hers.

Jared left that instant, calling to Gran that he needed to go, running out the door and taking off in his truck, his belly fisting with dread as he prayed he was wrong about who he thought that voice belonged to.

Chapter Twelve

Annette had been gripping her cell phone in her hand when it rang.

Without thinking of the consequences, she pressed the answer button on the sly, hoping Brett wouldn't notice.

But he saw what she'd done, and he grabbed the phone, tossing it away.

At least he hadn't taken the time to disconnect the call as he raised his voice to her. "Did you really think I wouldn't notice you were gone, Annette?"

She recognized this man through and through. This was the Calm-Before-the-Storm Brett who'd tried to reason with her after she'd seen him kissing her brides-maid in his dressing room.

And the guy who'd turned into something much worse when he'd lifted a hand to hit Annette after she told him that she wasn't going to marry him.

"Really," he continued calmly, although with a more aggressive tone than normal, "it hurts that you're surprised to see me. Didn't you think I cared enough to find out where you went?"

She merely watched him as he stood in the home she'd nested in after escaping him. He was still as handsome as an all-American quarterback, with his perfectly cut sandy hair, piercing blue eyes, male-model jaw and weekend-at-the-resort shirt and khakis.

The complete opposite of Jared, she thought. In so many ways.

He was tense, and she got the feeling that if she said the wrong thing, he might lash out, grab on to her arm, force her out of the door with him to who knew where.

So she remained collected. "I don't want any trouble, Brett."

"I'm not here to make trouble." He scanned her with his gaze, then frowned as he came to her tummy. "You're...pregnant."

"Yes." She swallowed. "There's a man I met here, and we—"

"Don't lie to me, Annette."

She shook her head, sensing his temper escalating. "I'm not lying. Brett, you never loved me, and when I realized that, I found comfort in the only way I could."

Lies, lies, lies.

Please believe them, she thought.

But did he? Because he didn't say so, one way or another. Maybe he didn't even care about having a baby with her except for it being something he needed to do as a husband, just to show the world he was a perfect Cresswell. During their short engagement he'd never talked with any enthusiasm about having kids, although, for a brief time, she'd believed that news of her pregnancy might set a spark to life in him.

But she'd never told him, thank God.

He was still looking at her stomach, and she distracted him.

"If you loved me so much," she said, "why did it take you so long to find me?"

He stuck his hands in his pockets, but they were fisted.

She didn't like his silence. "It's been months since I left," she continued. "Did you hire a P.I. and he ran into stumbling blocks? Or did it just take a while for you to do the hiring?"

A small you-got-me smile lifted the corner of his mouth. So he *hadn't* rushed to find out where she'd gone. Something had changed his mind about tracking her down.

"You always were perceptive," he finally said. "Maybe a little too much so, but you made me a promise, Annette. And it embarrassed the hell out of me when you didn't keep it."

"You made me a promise, too, or did you forget it when you helped yourself to a bridesmaid?"

She should've just kept that last remark to herself because his gaze darkened.

"You know," he said, "at first, I told my dad that it was for the best that you left. Yeah, you tore apart my pride, but it was easy to announce to the wedding guests that you were ill. You weren't around to tell anyone differently, and when, afterward, I made it known that *I* broke off the marriage, I thought I could live with that. I was fine with finding someone new. Someone who didn't have it in her to disappoint me like you did."

"Then why did you come here?"

"Because, according to my dad, I must've done something to run you off. He and my mom genuinely liked you, Annette. Your family had a good name, even if they went broke. You were like Princess Di to them— sweet, charitable, beautiful enough to garner positive attention in the society column."

How had she never seen through this guy? "That's why you're here? Because your parents approved of me?"

"Not exactly." He removed his hands from his pockets and casually folded his arms over his chest. "Let me ask you this—if someone wronged you and got away with it, would you stand for that?"

Oh, God. He didn't want her back at all, did he? He wanted something altogether different, although she wasn't sure what it was yet.

It was too bad she hadn't seen his true colors until their wedding day, when she'd realized that Brett didn't think like a lot of other men. Even though his parents seemed kind, they had clearly spoiled him, brought him up in some way that made him believe he could take whatever he wanted...including a belated trip to see her.

"Okay," she said, trying to steady her voice, thinking of the phone in the corner. Hopefully whoever had called was listening in and getting help. "It sounds as if you were going to let me off the hook at first. What changed your mind?"

"The thought of finishing what you started."

She started to inch to the side, toward the door.

He went on. "My reputation didn't really suffer after the wedding. We did some very good spin doctoring. But, as the months passed, what you did to me started to eat away at my gut. I knew a man would never take what you'd dished out, so I called a P.I."

He held up a hand in a gesture that caused her to halt in her tracks. He had noticed what she was doing.

"I'm not here to hurt you, Annette."

That didn't make her feel any better. Still, she tried to reason with him.

"Don't you understand why I left?"

He gave her a "because you overreacted about the bridesmaid" look. "Listen, I just thought I knew you better than I really did. All the people we're acquainted with have understandings in their marriages. It's no secret in the circles I run in, at least. I don't know about yours. Besides, I thought your parents had the same arrangement mine did, and you were savvy enough to realize what would be expected."

"No. My parents were never like that." Had she been ultra-naïve about the high society world she'd supposedly been a part of? Her mom had never told her to expect a lying, cheating dog of a husband.

If Mom had been alive to meet Brett, she might've seen through him and warned Annette away.

"Wow," Brett said, laughing. "See, I just assumed you were up to speed on all that. I was pretty certain you were more worldly."

She tried to see in him what had drawn her in the first place—his charm, his smile, his manners and philanthropic pursuits. But they'd all been so superficial.

She hadn't looked deeply enough, as she'd gotten the opportunity to do with Jared.

Jared…

Out of the corner of her eye, she saw her phone on

the carpet. Was it too much to hope that the caller had been Jared?

Brett gestured toward her stomach. "Are you sure this isn't mine?"

"I told you that she isn't," Annette said, attempting not to sound desperate, but sweat was starting to bead up on her skin.

He frowned, and for a moment, she wondered if he was rethinking his trip down here. She knew that Brett was too proud to raise another man's child as his own, so she hoped that he would want nothing to do with her daughter.

Annette shifted position again. The door didn't seem too far away. "I'm not worth the effort you're taking. I don't know exactly what you want from me, but—"

"I want you to know that there are consequences for leaving me at the altar."

"But you said—"

"I said my pride smarted when I let you go at first. But I also said a man shouldn't stand for the way you treated me."

She'd narrowed her eyes when he'd described himself as a man. A man was someone who owned up to his wrongs, who tried to correct them. Someone like Jared, who'd sent her that text this morning that had opened his emotions wide.

Her expression had obviously pushed a button in Brett, and he stepped toward her, getting close to her face.

"Don't you ever look at me as if you're above me." He nearly growled the words in a dark, rumbling tone.

Then he peered down at her stomach again, leveling

out his voice. It wasn't any less scary, though. Actually, this kind of calm from Brett was far more frightening.

"Annette," he said, "all you have to do is come back to Tulsa with me. Not for a marriage but to do your own kind of damage control."

"I thought you already took care of that."

The PR the Cresswells had done obviously wasn't enough. Brett wanted a pound of social flesh.

He and his ego wanted satisfaction.

"I need you to show yourself around town," he said. Then he gestured toward her sweater and sweatpants. "I'd like everyone to see you in these clothes you're wearing now as you tell them that you want me back."

She could appease him by saying yes just to get out of this situation, or she could tell him to go to hell.

The choice would've been easy if she didn't have a baby between them.

"Annette." The scary voice returned as he backed her against the wall.

She held up her hands, her pulse skittering, telling her to run again, to try and—

The sound of a key in the front door startled her as she and Brett whipped their gazes over to the entry, where someone was coming in.

As the door creaked open, a tall man dressed in black stood, his arms at his sides.

Jared's blood curdled at the sight of the blond man cornering Annette and her unborn baby.

When she saw him, her eyes were wide with not only relief but more. So much more.

A flash of the past rolled over Jared's mind—Tessa Hadenfield in her house that night, threatened by the thugs, just before Tony had saved her. She'd been pregnant, too, that night, even if it hadn't been obvious to anyone.

But Tony had given everything for the woman he loved and their child, Jared thought. And, like Tony, *he* was going to be Annette's hero, and not just for today, either.

Raw emotion made him spring at the intruder just as he was backing away from Annette. But Jared caught him, grabbing him by the shirt, shoving him into the kitchen.

"You all right?" he asked Annette while still glaring at Brett. He'd been listening to her phone call on speakerphone all the way here, so he knew everything that had happened.

"I'm good," she said.

He walked toward Brett, who was just as tall, just as built but not half as motivated. Jared shoved Brett backward again, and he hit the refrigerator.

"You like picking on women?" Jared asked.

Brett raised his hands. So he was a lover, not a fighter?

"This is my fiancée," he said.

Jared actually laughed at that. "I don't think so."

"You the baby's father?" Brett asked.

Without hesitation, Jared said, "Yeah. I sure as hell am."

Now that this guy had been painted into a corner, Jared could see his dander rising.

But Brett was nothing to Jared, not after he'd spent years busting broncs. This kid was a prancing pony compared to them.

Jared hovered, an inch from Brett's face. "If you want to draw my blood for a DNA test, just go ahead."

Brett seemed somewhat relieved by the strong words and the confidence Jared had that the baby was his. Good, because now, more than ever, Jared wanted to be the one who would get to see the baby grow in Annette's tummy, see her born, see her every day for the rest of his life.

Time to end this. Jared took him by the shirt again and hauled him toward the door. But before he threw him out, he said, "Do I need to ask if you're gonna leave us alone?"

"I—"

"I'd hate for you to operate under the impression that you had any rights whatsoever to a woman and baby who aren't yours."

Brett got a rebellious gleam in his gaze. "I don't think you know who you're dealing with."

"Sure I do. And I think the slime I'm dealing with has a reputation in Tulsa society he kind of enjoys, right?"

Brett's smile told Jared that he was indeed correct. He had a reputation. But Jared wasn't talking about the kind that would scare people off with threats of what he could accomplish with his money.

He was talking about a vulnerability.

"I like men who value their reputations," he said. "They have something to defend. Just how precious is your reputation to you, Brett?"

Before he could answer, Annette spoke up from behind them. "Precious enough so that he came down here to preserve it. He wanted me to do an apology tour in Tulsa."

"So I heard." Jared shook his head. "A reputation's a hard thing to maintain, especially if it's been highly polished over the generations. I wonder how happy your dad would be if some of my reporter friends got wind of a tasty little scandal like this. A society creep who chases down women and unleashes his temper on them. Sounds like one of those pieces of crap you'd see on *Nightline*."

It took Brett only a hot second to recognize that Jared wasn't BSing him.

"Just remember," Jared said quietly, "I've got my friends on speed dial."

He opened the door for Brett, and the man walked out. But he glanced over his shoulder on the way, as Jared started to follow him.

"I didn't want her back anyway," he said. "Just look at her—a small-town slob. That's what she's turned into."

Jared started to walk toward Brett, but the other man continued to the parking lot. It wasn't until Jared saw him get in his Porsche and drive off that he went back inside.

Annette was waiting for him, but neither of them made a move toward each other.

Jared felt his blood go cold. Fear crawled up his spine. When they'd last been together, they had argued. He'd sent that text and she'd never answered.

Was everything going to be okay between them or had she—

She rushed into his arms, embracing him as if she would die before ever letting him go anywhere again. He let loose the breath he'd been holding and returned the hug tenfold, burying his face in her hair, choked with emotion.

"I hope you didn't take anything he said to heart," he murmured.

"The small-town-slob comment?" she asked, laughing into his chest. "How can I feel inferior when I have you?"

She stood on her tiptoes and kissed him as if he were her entire life. As if he were all the hero a woman could ever want.

He kissed her back, pressing his mouth to hers so hard that he was afraid he would bruise her. But, when he eased up, she deepened the kiss again, getting everything she could from him.

And he was willing to give it all.

They came up for air, and she said, "I'm so glad you came back, not only because he was here, but—"

"I was going to come back to you even before I heard you on the phone. That's why I made that call to you in the first place—so I could see if you'd still have me."

"Yes, I'll have you. I'm never letting you think that I want you to be anywhere but here, Jared."

He kept planting little kisses on her temple, her nose, her mouth again. She tasted so sweet, tasted like his.

Stroking her face, he looked her over.

"I told you I'm okay," she said.

"I'm just going to make sure of it. He didn't lay a hand on you?"

"No."

"Well, I'm taking you home with me tonight, just in case. I'm going to watch over you until I find out that Brett's back in Tulsa." He kissed her on the forehead. "In fact, I'd like to take you home forever, Annie."

Tears shone in her eyes. "Really?"

"You and our baby."

"Our...baby." A sob escaped her. "Are you sure about this?"

"One hundred percent."

She rubbed her face with her sweater, wiping her tears. "I had to lie to Brett so he'd doubt this child was his. I thought telling him that the baby was someone else's would turn him off."

"I'm sure he's never coming around again," he said. "As sure as the sun rises every morning. As sure as I am that I love you and I'm never going to stop loving you."

"I love you, too, Jared."

She kissed him again, and when they were done, he skimmed his lips to the corner of her mouth, to the little cove under her ear, to the curve of her neck.

Holding her tighter, he said, "When I walked in, I wanted to kill him. I'm sure Tony felt the same way when..."

He trailed off. Damn, he had a lot to tell her.

"Come here," he said, taking her hand and bringing her to the sofa, sitting her down with care.

They had a view of her backyard, the Valentine's Day sun shining down on the place where everything had taken root for them.

"When I walked in," he said again as he held her hand, "I saw Brett ready to hurt you. It reminded me of Tessa and Tony."

"How?"

He told her all about what Davis and Violet, then Gran, had related to him this morning. Told her how Tony, aka Sean Mullaney, had definitely been involved with Bugs Moran and the St. Valentine's Day Massacre. Told her what happened after Tony had met Tessa Hadenfield, and how he had died saving her.

"It turns out that a bad man can turn good," he said. "Or, maybe I should say that a good man turned bad man can go good."

Annette kissed him, cutting him off until they both needed to breathe again. She coasted her fingertips down his cheek, his neck, sending fierce vibrations through him.

"Didn't you say Gran wants you to keep these secrets in your family?" she whispered.

She was smiling, as if she knew what he was going to say to that.

"You are my family, Annie."

This time, their kiss opened up a new world, one in which the future was theirs.

Slowly, he slid her sweater over her head, her hair spilling out like pale sunshine that would color the rest of his days. He kissed her neck, her collarbone, right on down to the top of her breasts that mounded over her bra.

She moaned as he took his time exploring her, being gentle, undoing the bra and bringing her to longer, lower moans with his mouth on her nipples.

As she lay on her back, arching toward him, he worked off her sweatpants, her panties. He touched her between her legs, sliding his finger between her folds, then into her.

She was being louder now, and he watched her face, his belly tightening at the pleasure he saw there.

Then his clothing was on the floor next to hers, and she was ready for him.

"Come over here," she said, pulling him to her as he positioned himself carefully over her.

He put a pillow under her back as she rested against the arm of the couch, and he entered her, bringing one of her legs up to his side, opening her wider for him as her moans turned into throaty cries.

Straining, he filled her, just as she filled him, and it was as if time swirled around them, sweeping them to another place.

A place where nothing but sunshine existed, bathing him until it got so hot that he felt as if he were melting.

Liquefying.

Pooling like wax from a burning candle and then hardening again as his body climaxed.

He spilled into her, unable to breathe, unable to do any more than hold her and help her to her own climax with his fingers, his mouth.

His everything.

Timeless, he thought, kissing her again. They were as timeless as any true love.

And just as complete.

Epilogue

Heartbreak Hill's lonely view of St. Valentine wasn't as lonely as usual today.

Not with a good deal of the town here, gathered under the spring sun, cheering while Jared Colton took Annette Olsen as his wife.

As the ceremony ended, they kissed amid a shower of rose petals that four-year-old Kristy Flannigan, their flower girl, impulsively tossed into the air.

The first thing Jared did after he hugged his wife to him, whispering "I love you" into her ear, was open his arms so that Gran, their matron of honor, could bring his and Annette's new daughter to them.

Angelica Colton, who was swaddled in a lacy white blanket, merely pursed her lips and fisted her little hands as he and Annette held her and their guests hooted and hollered some more.

Jared kissed his daughter, loving her baby smell, before Annette did the same. Then they handed her back to Gran so they could take a run down the grassy aisle.

At the end of it, Rita and Conn Flannigan, whom they'd gotten to know well these past few months, met them.

"Congratulations!" they said, hugging the bride and groom.

Rita looked as if her tummy was about to pop, she was so big, and ready to have this baby any minute, it seemed.

Soon, Annette and Jared were surrounded by well-wishers: Annette's friends from Tulsa, whom she'd been able to invite now that she didn't have to keep her location a secret from Brett anymore. Aaron Rhodes, the rugged president of the chamber of commerce. Rita's rancher brother and sister, Nick and Kim. Margery Wilmore and her joyful sobbing. Terry—Annette's manager—and the rest of the staff from the diner, which had closed for the day. The Chess Nerds were there, too, looking as jovial as could be, and so were a few ex-miners who'd introduced themselves to Jared the past few months, officially welcoming him to St. Valentine.

Davis and Violet Jackson came to the reception circle at the end, after everyone else had retreated to the buffet tables that had already been laid out by the caterers. Jared and Annette hadn't seen any sense in having everyone wait to celebrate.

Davis shook Jared's hand. "All the best to you two."

Annette had just finished hugging Violet, and she went for Davis now. "You two found the best in each other, just like us. I guess that makes us a club of sorts."

As Violet started to compliment Annette on how

svelte she looked in what Annette had described to Jared as a "slim gossamer chiffon gown with cap sleeves," he and Davis looked on.

"This day wouldn't have been as happy without your help," Jared said. "We appreciate all you've done."

Not only had Davis and Violet kept tabs on Brett's social life in Tulsa, thanks to some journalist contacts there, but there'd been the matter of Tony, too.

"Don't even mention it," Davis said.

"You've been real stand-up about everything."

"Hey, *The Recorder* never publishes stories unless the facts are straight."

With one glance, Jared saw that Davis meant it. He and Violet had never published what they knew about Tony Amati/Sean Mullaney, and Jared had never broken his vow to Gran about divulging the secrets about Tony and Tessa. Even so, Jared had no doubt that Davis knew there was more to the tale, but St. Valentine was already in the flush without having to exploit Tony. The recent Cowboy Festival had lured more crowds than they'd known what to do with, and it promised to be a lucrative venture for years to come.

Jared had even covered up the holes he'd dug in Annette's garden, leaving the past where it belonged.

Violet had evidently caught wind of the conversation, and she came to Davis, her hand on her belly.

"I'm actually glad the investigation is over," she said. "We're going to need time for ourselves."

"Are you...?" Annette asked.

Both Davis and Violet nodded, and Davis said, "I guess I'll be asking Jared for fathering tips."

After more congratulations all around, Jared stole

Annette away, heading for the copse of trees that offered the best view of St. Valentine.

"Alone at last," he said.

"Not for too long." Annette held her veil to her head as a gentle wind combed over them, whistling and rustling the spring leaves. "I can't wait to meet Melissa."

Jared merely nodded, unable to speak. After Valentine's Day, when everything had seemed new and possible with Annette at his side, he had gathered his courage and contacted his ex-wife, asking if it would be okay to do more than send money for his daughter every month.

Gradually, he had gotten to know his eleven-year-old over the phone and through email, and she had asked to meet him in Reno, where they'd moved years ago. Jared and Annette had decided to make it a part of their honeymoon, and they would introduce Angelica while they were at it. He would have invited Melissa to the wedding, but Joelle had said it was too soon, and he had respected that.

He nuzzled Annette's cheek. "Melissa's going to think the world of you."

As the wind kept playing around them, it almost felt as if there was another presence here. A superstitious man would've thought it was Tony, if the town founder really was buried up here somewhere.

Annette must've felt it, too. "I wish they could've been as happy in the end as we are."

"Who knows? Maybe they are."

Annette got a glint in her blue eyes, and she started plucking petals from her bouquet.

"What're you doing?"

"Making things right." She gave a few petals to him,

then closed her eyes. "Can't you see them, Jared? Standing together, watching us, blessing us?"

Yes, he could, now that he'd closed his eyes, too, and put his mind to imagining. He saw Tony dressed in the suit and vest that he wore in most of his old-time pictures in town, with a watch fob hanging from his pocket. And he saw his great-grandma Tessa with a sparkle in her eyes as she linked arms with the love of her life.

When Jared felt a shower of petals come down around him, he realized that Annette had thrown some in the air, just as if Tony and Tessa had gotten married and Jared and Annette were here to cheer them on.

He tossed up his petals, too. A benediction. A cleansing.

For all of them.

In his mind, he saw Tony looking at him with his dark eyes, nodding, acknowledging his great-grandson—a part of something bigger than what Jared had ever dreamed possible.

I finally came home, Tony, he thought. *And you're the one who brought me here.*

When he opened his eyes, Tony and Tessa were gone, and he only saw his own bride, Annette, who smiled just before she fell into his arms, squeezing him, loving him.

Yes, he'd finally come home to her arms, Jared thought, embracing her with all the love he'd discovered here in St. Valentine.

And in the woman he would love forever.

* * * * *

COMING NEXT MONTH
from Harlequin® Special Edition®
AVAILABLE FEBRUARY 19, 2013

#2245 ONE LESS LONELY COWBOY

Kathleen Eagle

Cowboy Jack McKenzie has a checkered past, but when rancher's daughter Lily reluctantly visits her father, he wants more than anything to show that he's a reformed man. Has she made up her mind too early that this would be a short stay at the ranch?

#2246 A SMALL FORTUNE

The Fortunes of Texas: Southern Invasion

Marie Ferrarella

After a broken marriage, Asher Fortune moves to Red Rock, where he needs someone to help him and his four-year-old son, Jace, start a new life. He knew upon their first meeting that Marnie was great for Jace, but he didn't realize what was in store for *him!*

#2247 HOW TO CATCH A PRINCE

Royal Babies

Leanne Banks

Hardworking Maxwell Carter has just found out he's the son of the ruling prince of Chantaine, and he's been convinced by his dependable assistant, Sophie, to visit his newfound family. They see the potential sparks between the two immediately, but can a royal makeover by his half sisters help this plain Jane catch the prince's heart for good?

#2248 THE RIGHT TWIN

Gina Wilkins

Aaron Walker retreats to the Bell Resort to escape the pressure of his overachieving family's expectations, only to find his highly successful twin already there, stealing the spotlight as usual! But the beautiful Shelby Bell has eyes only for the restless and shy twin, and will do what it takes to convince him that she is exactly what he has been looking for all his life.

#2249 TAMMY AND THE DOCTOR

Byrds of a Feather

Judy Duarte

Cowgirl Tammy Byrd has always been a tomboy, outroping and outriding all the men on the ranch. Until Dr. Mike Sanchez presents her with a whole new challenge that doesn't involve getting her hands dirty. Can she learn to let her hair down—and lasso the man of her dreams?

#2250 DADDY SAYS, "I DO!"

The Pirelli Brothers

Stacy Connelly

When Kara Starling takes her nephew to meet the father he's never known, she doesn't expect Sam Pirelli to be the perfect daddy. And she certainly never guessed that he could also be the perfect man for her!

You can find more information on upcoming Harlequin® titles, free excerpts and more at www.HarlequinInsideRomance.com.

HSECNM0213

REQUEST YOUR FREE BOOKS!

2 FREE NOVELS PLUS 2 FREE GIFTS!

H HARLEQUIN®

SPECIAL EDITION

Life, Love & Family

YES! Please send me 2 FREE Harlequin® Special Edition novels and my 2 FREE gifts (gifts are worth about $10). After receiving them, if I don't wish to receive any more books, I can return the shipping statement marked "cancel." If I don't cancel, I will receive 6 brand-new novels every month and be billed just $4.49 per book in the U.S. or $5.24 per book in Canada. That's a savings of at least 14% off the cover price! It's quite a bargain! Shipping and handling is just 50¢ per book in the U.S. and 75¢ per book in Canada.* I understand that accepting the 2 free books and gifts places me under no obligation to buy anything. I can always return a shipment and cancel at any time. Even if I never buy another book, the two free books and gifts are mine to keep forever.

235/335 HDN FVTV

Name _____ (PLEASE PRINT) _____

Address _____ Apt. # _____

City _____ State/Prov. _____ Zip/Postal Code _____

Signature (if under 18, a parent or guardian must sign) _____

Mail to the **Harlequin® Reader Service:**
IN U.S.A.: P.O. Box 1867, Buffalo, NY 14240-1867
IN CANADA: P.O. Box 609, Fort Erie, Ontario L2A 5X3

Want to try two free books from another line?
Call 1-800-873-8635 or visit www.ReaderService.com.

* Terms and prices subject to change without notice. Prices do not include applicable taxes. Sales tax applicable in N.Y. Canadian residents will be charged applicable taxes. Offer not valid in Quebec. This offer is limited to one order per household. Not valid for current subscribers to Harlequin Special Edition books. All orders subject to credit approval. Credit or debit balances in a customer's account(s) may be offset by any other outstanding balance owed by or to the customer. Please allow 4 to 6 weeks for delivery. Offer available while quantities last.

Your Privacy—The Harlequin® Reader Service is committed to protecting your privacy. Our Privacy Policy is available online at www.ReaderService.com or upon request from the Harlequin Reader Service.

We make a portion of our mailing list available to reputable third parties that offer products we believe may interest you. If you prefer that we not exchange your name with third parties, or if you wish to clarify or modify your communication preferences, please visit us at www.ReaderService.com/consumerschoice or write to us at Harlequin Reader Service Preference Service, P.O. Box 9062, Buffalo, NY 14269. Include your complete name and address.

HSEI3

*In Buckshot Hills, Texas, a sexy doctor meets his match
in the least likely woman—a beautiful cowgirl looking to
reinvent herself....*

Enjoy a sneak peek from USA TODAY *bestselling author
Judy Duarte's new Harlequin® Special Edition® story,*
TAMMY AND THE DOCTOR ,*the first book in
Byrds of a Feather, a brand-new miniseries launching
in March 2013!*

***

Before she could comment or press Tex for more details, a
couple of light knocks sounded at the door.

Her grandfather shifted in his bed, then grimaced. "Who
is it?"

"Mike Sanchez."

Doc? Tammy's heart dropped to the pit of her stomach
with a thud, then thumped and pumped its way back up
where it belonged.

"Come on in," Tex said.

Thank goodness her grandfather had issued the invitation, because she couldn't have squawked out a single word.

As Doc entered the room, looking even more handsome
than he had yesterday, Tammy struggled to remain cool and
calm.

And it wasn't just her heartbeat going wacky. Her femi-
nine hormones had begun to pump in a way they'd never
pumped before.

"Good morning," Doc said, his gaze landing first on Tex,
then on Tammy.

As he approached the bed, he continued to look at Tammy,

his head cocked slightly.

"What's the matter?" she asked.

"I'm sorry. It's just that your eyes are an interesting shade of blue. I'm sure you hear that all the time."

"Not really." And not from anyone who'd ever mattered. In truth, they were a fairly common color—like the sky or bluebonnets or whatever. "I've always thought of them as run-of-the-mill blue."

"There's nothing ordinary about it. In fact, it's a pretty shade."

The compliment set her heart on end. But before she could think of just the perfect response, he said, "If you don't mind stepping out of the room, I'd like to examine your grandfather."

Of course she minded leaving. She wanted to stay in the same room with Doc for the rest of her natural-born days. But she understood her grandfather's need for privacy.

"Of course." Apparently it was going to take more than simply batting her eyes to woo him, but there was no way Tammy would be able to pull off a makeover by herself. Maybe she could ask her beautiful cousins for help?

She had no idea what to say the next time she ran into them. But somehow, by hook or by crook, she'd have to think of something.

Because she was going to risk untold humiliation and embarrassment by begging them to turn a cowgirl into a lady!

***

Look for TAMMY AND THE DOCTOR from
Harlequin® Special Edition® available March 2013

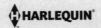

SPECIAL EDITION

Life, Love and Family

Coming in March 2013 from fan-favorite author

KATHLEEN EAGLE

Cowboy Jack McKenzie has a checkered past,
but when rancher's daughter Lily reluctantly visits her
father, he wants more than anything to show that
he's a reformed man. Has she made up her mind too
early that this would be a short stay at the ranch?

Look for *One Less Lonely Cowboy*
next month from Kathleen Eagle.

*Available March 2013 from Harlequin Special Edition
wherever books are sold.*

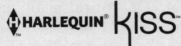